IRRELEPHANT OMENS

MAGICAL MIDWAY PARANORMAL COZY SERIES, BOOK #5

LEANNE LEEDS

BADCHEN PUBLISHING

Irrelephant Omens
Published by Badchen Publishing
14125 W State Highway 29
Suite B-203 119
Liberty Hill, TX 78642 USA

IRRELEPHANT OMENS

CHAPTER 1

"NOW, LOOK HERE, YOUNG MAN!" ETHEL ELKINS screeched. She sat at one end of a large wooden table. Devana sat beside her (as always), a concerned look on her face and a comforting hand on the old lady's shoulder. "This isn't some negotiation to be had! This is a straight-up brawl, and Charlotte needs to—"

"With all due respect, ma'am, it is our job to *share* the information we have access to with Charlotte and her group," Aidan told her calmly from the opposite end of the table. "The decision is not ours to make. We are not generals of an army. We are important consultants, but consultants only."

"Don't you tell me what I am!" Ethel Elkins

shouted. Her fleshy fist pounded the wooden table. I jumped, but Aidan remained relaxed and unconcerned even as Ethel was furious and frustrated.

We had gathered around the large table to discuss a strategy for dealing with the Witches' Council. Gunther and I, Fiona and Ningul, Aidan and Kyle, Ethel Elkins and Devana. Fortuna Delphi, the only member of our party not paired up, sat alone in the corner watching the argument between Ms. Elkins and Aidan. Her eyes were as wide as saucers.

Nine paranormals sat around a table on a Saturday night trying to pick a way forward.

"I don't think shouting at Aidan is going to accomplish anything," Gunther told the old woman.

"She doesn't care if it's going to accomplish anything," Cama, a mysterious bat that joined us when we visited my parents in Mickwac, Texas, tittered with what sounded like a laugh. "That old woman has been screaming for at *least* a millennium. I doubt she even knows how to talk anymore at a level that doesn't split mortal ears."

This shouting match is unlikely to be productive, Samson thought. He sat in my lap. *With the*

Witches' Council meeting next week, you are running out of time.

The only one at the table doing the shouting was Ethel Elkins and so far, from what I had seen? No one could calm her down.

A year ago I was an introverted, quiet homebody.

Now *I* was the unelected general in some paranormal tug-of-war over the fate of the world.

Despite growing up a witch and knowing that my family owned one of the few traveling paranormal circuses, those two facts never played that large of a role in my life. I knew my parents were witches, we had specific abilities that were somewhat entertaining and useful, but beyond that, I didn't really think about it much. The family animal shelter and the rescue of abused and abandoned pets played a more significant role in my life than the Magical Midway.

All that changed when my Uncle Phil died and passed the circus to me.

It was at that point I realized that *maybe* I should have paid more attention to this paranormal stuff.

"It must be Charlotte's choice, that's all I'm saying," Aidan said to the assembled group.

"When she inherited the power of the Magical Midway, she inherited the choice."

"I'm not the only ringmaster in the paranormal world, Aidan," I pointed out. "If this inherited choice is a ringmaster power, we really should have Roland Makepeace here to discuss the situation. What if I get all this information, make a decision, and then he chooses something different?"

"He doesn't matter," Ethel Elkins declared, waving her hand.

"I think my father might argue that opinion, ma'am," Gunther told the old woman.

Gunther, my boyfriend, was the heir apparent to the only *other* paranormal circus left on the entire planet. Currently, though, his father held the ringmaster position—and the superpowers that made Roland Makepeace one of the two most powerful witches on earth.

I was the other one.

Despite my plethora of powers, however, I couldn't get my squabbling group to stop arguing.

"I don't care *what* your father wants to argue, he still *doesn't matter*," Ms. Elkins told him.

"I keep telling you that you keep saying that people don't matter, and everyone matters, lady," Cama clicked and squeaked. "You are a very stubborn norn. Stubborn, stubborn, stubborn as the day is long, long, long. And you wonder why *you* don't get to choose. Humph."

"I don't wonder that!"

"Uh huh," Cama said with as much insincerity as a squeaking bat could muster.

"Only the thirteenth witch matters, only those of the proper generation matter, and only those destined to make a choice and aid in the choice matter," Devana stated quietly. "That is Ms. Elkins' perspective. It is difficult for her to consider those that don't have a role to play in the future. She doesn't intend to say that they don't matter as people, Cama. Just that they are not… consequential in what is to come."

The huntress witch rarely smiled. She was always serious. Out of the strange beings that I had met in the year since I became ringmaster, Devana was perhaps the most frightening of them all. I just couldn't figure her out, but I sensed how deadly she was. It radiated off of her forcefully like a warning.

"I don't even see how that's possible," I told the terrifying huntress witch. "The meeting with the Witches' Council is *next week*, and Roland Makepeace is the other ringmaster *this week*."

"Things change," Ms. Elkins snapped. Devana placed a hand on her shoulder again.

"Not *that* much, it seems," I told her, and she rolled her eyes.

"I feel like I've been hit by a truck," I told Gunther. We hid in my studio off the main great room in what *used* to be *my* yurt.

Now it was like a sleepaway camp cabin for squabbling supernatural beings.

"At least your uncle is able to take care of the Magical Midway issues while we focus on this." Gunther sat down on the futon. "Just think of how worn out you would feel if you had to manage all the operational stuff for the Magical Midway as well as this group of plotting paranormals."

"I wonder if Uncle Phil and I can trade jobs for a couple of days?"

"I don't think it works that way, unfortunately." Gunther smiled.

"I'm starting to think *nobody* knows how it works," I told my boyfriend and plopped down on the futon next to him. "This is the most disorganized, argumentative group of people I have *ever* had to deal with. They think I'm predestined to make some major decision, but they don't know what it is. Ms. Elkins thinks I should just do what she tells me, and Aidan's contribution to the discussion is for me to *not* do what Ms. Elkins tells me."

"That actually does sum it up quite well." Gunther smiled again.

"With all of this fighting over a decision they *won't* tell me about, though, I don't feel like I'm getting any useful information."

"Remember, they're not infallible...but they probably like to *think* they are," Gunther pointed out. He tapped his hand on my shoulder and motioned for me to turn around. I felt my hair gently moved off my shoulders, and gentle fingers pressed against my tense muscles.

"Oh, wow, that feels incredible."

While Gunther rubbed the knots out of my neck, he continued. "My guess is they're not telling you about the decision you're going to be presented with because they don't *know* what that decision is."

"A fat lot of good they're doing me, then," I mumbled into the hair that had fallen across my face. Gunther's ministrations slowly melted the stress from my neck and shoulders. My head flopped forward and bounced on my chest.

"Feeling any better?"

"My neck and shoulders? Absolutely. About our ragtag coven? Not so much."

"Can you read anything from them beyond what they're saying?"

"From Aidan, absolutely," I told Gunther, turning back to face him. "Aidan feels the same as he always did. He just *is* who he is with a lot more knowledge than he used to have, you know? Ms. Elkins, on the other hand, I just can't figure out."

"I wish my mother were here," Gunther sighed. "My dad always had her deal with Ms. Elkins because…actually, I have no idea why she was always the one dealing with her. But Mom always handled anything about Ms. Elkins' concerns or problems. My mother would know what to do."

Gunther winced.

It was a subtle, tiny flicker of tension I recognized. Each time Gunther brought up his mother, a momentary flash of grief seemed to cut through him like a knife. He took the flash like a body blow, and then the moment passed.

Even though she had been killed twenty years before, Gunther still felt it.

Months ago, I learned that the Witches' Council was behind the murder of Mrs. Makepeace. It was a secret I had kept from Gunther, one fact in a stack of facts about the Witches' Council that I filed away to help me figure out what I would do. At the time I found out, I wasn't entirely sure I could trust Gunther, and so I had said nothing.

Once we became closer?

Admittedly, I probably should have told him then.

I justified keeping the secret by telling myself I had no proof it was true. It was just an allegation. With no evidence and without his mother's murder directly affecting what we were doing…well, there didn't seem any point in saying anything.

I would accomplish nothing by telling Gunther—other than hurting him and opening old wounds.

"Maybe we should talk to your dad? Perhaps he has some insight he remembers from back then? Because if we *don't* figure out a way to bring her combat level down to a two from a ten, we are never going to get anything accomplished. We're just going to continue to be the audience that witnesses a daily throwdown between the past and the future."

"My dad's been doing really well lately." Gunther shifted uncomfortably on the futon. "Bringing up my mom? That has a tendency to make him...not do...very well."

"What do you mean 'not well'?"

"You met him when you first became ringmaster," he told me. I nodded. "The more pain he's in, the meaner he gets. I'm not trying to say he's a bad person or anything, but...He's been a powerful ringmaster for a long time, Charlotte. Powerful people that have had tragedies in their lives? Tragedies that deeply wounded them? They can become ruthless. He has a tendency to be ruthless. Right now he's not. I'd like to keep it that way."

"I get it. I take it he's not drinking anymore, either?"

"No, not at all." Gunther smiled proudly. "I think you turning me into a full witch and ensuring that he can pass on the ringmaster power to me was a *big* deal for him. It helped him resolve a lot of his anger."

"Well, he and I *both* turned you into a full witch," I disagreed. "I could not have done it on my own. Both of us *had* to join forces, or we never could have done it."

You know, you both know all this stuff, Samson, my sarcastic guardian, pointed out. *You have a week before the Witches' Council meeting. I would suggest the two of you stop meandering down memory lane and going over things done. Concentrate on the things you must do.*

I passed on Samson's observation, and Gunther nodded.

"I wish Samson weren't so defensive about telepathic communication with anyone besides me," I told Gunther while I scratched the black cat behind his ears. "I mean, I get why he is, but it sure would make it easier since you're here all the time if the two of you could talk to each other. I mean, since you have telepathic power, too."

Gunther's face dropped and he looked down in his lap. My eyes narrowed.

"Yeah, I've meant to talk to you about that," he said slowly. His eyes rose and met mine. "There's something about my telepathic power that I don't think you quite picked up on."

"Oh? what's that?"

Gunther stared at me and said nothing for the longest time. I could feel the emotions churning within him. He was worried about my reaction. I tried to pluck what he was trying to tell me out of his head, but he hid it beneath a mist of fear that obfuscated what he really thought.

"Gunther?"

Finally, he spoke.

"I don't have *telepathic power*," he said with a sigh. "I *only* have telepathic power with *you*."

Fortuna concentrated so hard that her hands shook. Exhaling loudly, her limbs relaxed. Opening her eyes, she looked at me and shook her head no.

"Powers don't work like this!" I exclaimed in frustration. "You either have the power, or you don't have the power! You can't have power with just *one person*. That's ridiculous! He must just be more comfortable with me, and so that's why it's stronger with me! Is he blocking it?"

You and I have powers only with each other, Samson pointed out.

But you're a guardian! You're a unique supernatural being or something!

So are you, Ringmaster. So is he as a ringmaster heir and lawgiver.

"I am so tired of these groundbreaking new

things happening with no explanation," I said out loud.

Perhaps you chose the wrong line of work, then, Samson said.

"I didn't *choose* this line of work, cat! I got teleported by your glowing butt to a clearing where I was told my ancestors, along with my uncle, chose me to run the Magical Midway! *I* was chosen, *not* the other way around."

If I recall, you agreed. That is a choice.

"Charlotte, maybe we should ask Aidan if this has happened in the past. Perhaps there's a reason for it," Fortuna pointed out. "Could lawgivers have the ability to telepathically speak only to one another?"

"I don't think his power works like that," I disagreed. "Besides, Aidan's been around Gunther since they met back in Mickwac. He hasn't said anything at all about Gunther's power being weird. Maybe he just needs to try harder."

"It's possible that it's *not* weird," Fortuna said.

"How is this not weird?"

"I am going to ask Aidan if he would be willing to join us," Fortuna said as she shot Gunther, who sat silently on the futon, a supportive look. With a quick smile at me, she ran out the door.

"How could you not tell me this beforehand?" I whirled on Gunther.

"It took me quite a bit of time to realize that your thoughts were the only thoughts I heard," Gunther told me a bit defensively. "I wasn't trying to keep something from you, Charlotte. I was just—"

"Enjoying the fact that more magic indicated we were bonded in some special way?"

Gunther winced like I'd slapped him. Sure, maybe what I said was a little bit unfair, but it's not like Gunther hadn't acted like some lovesick puppy dog before.

You can be very unfair when you are feeling defensive, Samson told me.

Be quiet. This doesn't concern you.

"That's not fair," Gunther replied as if he had heard Samson's thought. "You're assigning motivations to me because *you* are uncomfortable with the fact that someone believes we are destined to be together. Don't question *my* motivations or honesty with *you* simply because *you* have trouble being comfortable with the pro—"

"I'm not! That's not what I'm doing it all!"

"Isn't it, though?" Gunther sat back down. "If you want me to believe that *you're* not questioning me because of your own discomfort with the situation, I respectfully suggest you *stop* cutting off my words while I am speaking. Especially when you are doing it to tell me what *my* motivations are."

I groped through my angry and defensive brain looking for a snappy comeback, but I couldn't find one.

"Am I interrupting?" Aidan asked from the door.

"Why can't he read anyone's mind but mine?" I raged at Aidan.

"Because you're both lawgivers," Aidan answered calmly. "Were you both unaware that you are the only two lawgivers left?"

My jaw dropped, and Gunther sadly shook his head no.

"We knew there weren't many, but we didn't know we were the *only* two. Or maybe we did, but...I don't know that we stopped to think about it."

"The Witches' Council made sure that there were no lawgivers," Aidan told us as he made his way over to a chair in the sitting area. "If there were more lawgivers, they would be sitting on the Witches' Council as well. Clearly, they are not."

"What are lawgivers?" Kyle asked, poking his head in.

"The paranormal world's version of a police officer, I suppose," Aidan told his centaur ex-police officer boyfriend. "Charlotte and Gunther put on the lawgiver rings, and so they now operate as officers of justice after a fashion in our world."

"The two of them?" Kyle laughed and pointed. "*These two* are literally the *only* two cops you have to keep law and order? In the *entire* paranormal world?"

"It's a little more complicated than that. The Witches' Council has their own security force, but those law enforcement officers are not *lawgivers*. They don't have the power of the lawgiver ring, but they do have the political power of the Witches' Council behind them."

"But not the magical power they are supposed to have as representatives of justice," I added. "At least as the role was designed."

"That's because they're not justice seekers. They're simply enforcers of the Witches' Council's will," Gunther added.

"So if you have the ring, you're on the Witches' Council? Just like that?" Kyle asked.

"Lawgivers used to be a parliamentary body

that advised the Witches' Council as well as voted on issues," Aidan told him.

"That's amazing. Police officers helped make laws...I mean, that's kind of brilliant," Kyle mused. Then his face changed. "Frankly, that also sounds dangerous. What happens if you get a bunch of cops on the take? Laws can get twisted really fast when corruption takes hold."

"That's part of the power of the rings," Aidan told him. He pointed to my hand, and then Gunther's. "The rings don't enforce ethics, but they can *indicate* them. I suspect that's why the Witches' Council wanted to do away with the lawgivers in the first place."

"What do you mean 'indicate' them?" I asked, looking at the ring.

"Your ring is gold, and so your motives and ethics are pure. Well, at least as far as the magic of the ring can sense," Aidan told me. Gunther quickly looked at his own ring to ensure that it, too, was gold. "If your ring turns red, or black? I'd suggest a meditation on the righteousness of your intentions."

"What's the difference between black and red?" Gunther asked.

"Red means that your motivations are questionable. Your powers will be suspended, but the ring will remain on your finger in hopes that you can work through your issue and return the color to gold. If the ring turns black? Your lawgiver powers are removed forever, and the ring will fall off at the next rising of the sun. You have no recourse, and no way to come back from that. The magic has deemed you unrecoverable."

"I wish I'd had those back in Mickwac." Kyle stared wide-eyed at my ring.

"So it's an ethical mood ring?" I asked him.

"Perhaps a bit more complex than that, but that's an accurate way of putting it. In any case, your telepathic connection is because you're both lawgivers," Aidan said.

"And no more than that?" Gunther asked.

"Not that I'm aware of, no."

"I guess it's like a magical CB radio," I told Gunther.

"What's a CB radio?"

Everyone other than Gunther laughed.

"With so many paranormals from the human world, the human in-jokes are going to become a little bit annoying," Gunther grumbled.

CHAPTER 2

"Look, I *said* I was sorry." Gunther and I were walking around the fairgrounds. "I didn't mean to get accusatory, or defensive, or to impute anything."

"You did," Gunther disagreed. "You may not have intended to do those things, but you did those things, Charlotte."

I sighed and fell silent as we walked next to one another.

In a lot of ways, I liked Gunther better when he was handling me with kid gloves, hoping that I would love him back. Ever since I admitted I was in love with him? It seemed to have boosted his confidence in calling me on my stuff.

I wasn't used to it.

This intimate relationship honesty stuff could be tough.

"I'm not trying to punish you for your choices," Gunther told me. "As the months have passed, however, you have grown into your power as a ringmaster. I would only caution you that power has side effects. I have seen it with my father. Don't let it make you arrogant."

"I'm not arrogant!"

"No, not yet," Gunther smiled. "And *perhaps* not ever. But it's something you must guard against. Arrogance can take hold more easily than you think. Just look at Ms. Elkins."

I stopped walking and stared at my boyfriend. "You think I'm gonna turn into *her?*"

"I think you could," Gunther nodded. "And not because *you* are especially vulnerable to the arrogance that comes with power. I think you could only because power can corrupt if those who wield it are not constantly vigilant against its influence."

"Aidan got all his power all at once, and it didn't change him."

"Aidan got knowledge. *Not* power."

"Hey, knowledge is power!"

"Perhaps in your other world," Gunther said. "In the paranormal world, *power* is power.

Knowledge is simply knowledge, but it's meaningless if you don't do anything with it."

We continued advancing through the fairgrounds. I wiggled my fingers to address different issues I saw with the circus. Broken barrels here, a broken fence there, precariously stacked boxes on that shelf over there. Since I had brought the death bat to the Magical Midway, many of our citizens gave me a wide berth (coupled with suspicious glances from a distance). Today's maintenance walk indicated their concern level was still high. We ran into almost no one.

"I can't believe everybody so freaked out over a bat," I grumbled as I waved my hand and mended a canvas door across from the haunted house.

"Cama is not just a bat," Gunther reminded me.

"Right, right, it's a death bat, and if it steals a strand of your hair, you're gonna die, blah blah, yadda yadda," I told him quietly. "Compared to all of the other paranormals that we have here, and the Witches' Council continually breathing down our backs, I just don't see what makes Cama so much more frightening."

"I suspect it is the power to call her mother,"

Gunther said. "That, and normally when you come across a bat like her, she is an omen. Never a welcome one."

"Charlotte!" little Anna called from the haunted house door. The little ghost girl's head stuck out inches against the wooden barrier. "Charlotte! Charlotte! Charlotte! Mama says that it's time for Gunther to meet her! Can you two come? Can you come to meet Mama, Gunther?"

"I'd love to introduce the two of them," I called up. "We have time, sure."

"Her mother?" Gunther asked as we headed toward the haunted house entrance.

"I don't think the ghost is *really* her mother. Like, wasn't her mother when she was alive. I think she adopted Anna when she passed on because Anna didn't have anyone."

"That seems like a kind thing to do," Gunther said. We made our way up the steps.

"I'm amazed you didn't meet her when we were dealing with Tiffany Drake's ghost in Mickwac. Gerda is usually in the middle of everything that happens in that house, but for some reason, she never came out," I told him. A shadow passed across his face.

"The ghost's name is Gerda?" Gunther asked me in a strained voice.

"Yep, why?"

Gunther grabbed the door and held it open for me. The cool darkness and quiet reached out, and I felt the familiar peace take hold. A peace that melted away when I raised my eyes to Gunther's face. He was as pale as a...well, ghost.

"Gerda was my mother's name," Gunther told me.

Gerda the ghost shared a name with Gunther's mother because Gerda *was* the ghost of Gunther's mother. Great, fat, sparkling spectral tears rolled down her bright face as Gunther vibrated in shock.

"Son," Gerda whispered. "You have grown to be so handsome. I knew that you would be one of the kindest and most handsome of all the ringmasters one day."

"I don't understand," Gunther whispered, clutching my hand. He was squeezing so tightly that the invisible metallic shield encasing me clinked as he smashed my fingers together. "This can't be real. You're *not* real. This is some trick."

"It's no trick, my Gunther," Gerda told him. "There is much I must tell you about the coming storm. I have to explain why I've remained hidden from you, when I wished nothing more than to appear to you and tell you how much I love you, how proud I am of you. My beautiful son…"

Gerda moved slowly toward him, her hand outstretched. Anna watched with a beaming smile.

"Stop. Just stop," Gunther commanded her stepping backward. "Just stay back."

"Gunther, are you okay?" I asked him. I didn't know what else to do. I was feeling a pretty hefty dose of shock, myself. In all the months the ghost and I had spoken, she had never mentioned any of this to me.

"Charlotte, this is some Witches' Council trick," he told me. "My mother is *dead*. If she had stayed on this plane of existence as a ghost? She never would've left me alone for twenty years. She would've told me she was here. I don't know who this woman is, but it can't be my mother."

"Gunther—"

"You are not my mother!" Gunther cut Gerda off with a snarl. Sweat beaded against Gunther's red face as he stared in horror at the woman. "My mother *never would've left me alone to deal with an alcoholic father*! My mother never would've left me to defend myself against ridicule, ostracizing, and a *father that could never quite look at me because I looked too much like my dead human mother!*"

I looked back and forth between Gunther and Gerda. They looked almost exactly alike, clearly mother and son. The resemblance was unmistakable.

And yet...

I had been through this, though, with Faleena at the Werebear Jamboree. I knew that the Witches' Council had the power to make anyone look like anyone else. Ghosts had an inherent shapeshifting ability.

Gunther could be right. This could be a trick.

"Does he know that he's my brother, Mama?" Anna asked Gerda hopefully. The ghost child seemed oblivious to the trauma that Gunther was experiencing before our eyes. Or maybe she thought this news would make him happy.

"Get me out of here." Gunther grabbed my arm with his clammy hand. "I need to get away from that woman before I say something a child shouldn't hear."

"I'm over five hundred years old, big brother," Anna told him cheerfully. "There's not a lot that I haven't heard! Okay, well, *before* Tiffany Drake showed up, there were *a lot* of four-letter words that I hadn't heard, but I think she used them all when she was here. So *now* there's not a lot I haven't heard."

I had no doubt that Tiffany Drake had educated the small girl on a wide variety of curse words, unfortunately. I shuddered again as I remembered the dark shadow woman, Cama the death bat's feared mother, that took the teenage girl and her gangster father…somewhere.

"I have to go," Gunther whispered and dropped my arm. Turning away from the image of his mother and the eager face of his possible new sister, he ran out the door with a loud crash. I heard a sob escape from his throat just before the door slammed.

I stared after him, and then looked back at the stricken ghost I thought I had known. Anna's face shone with the hope of a child, still excited by the concept of a brother. Gerda stared into my eyes as I struggled with whether to stay or go. I had so many questions about what I just witnessed.

Yet I couldn't leave Gunther alone.

But I had to understand what had happened here.

I couldn't make my brain work well enough to come up with a question. I just stared at the ghost of Gerda Makepeace. She was beautiful. And the eyes staring back at me reminded me so much of Gunther's...

"I will be here, Charlotte." Gerda's outstretched hand fell and her head bowed. "Please, go to my son. Help him."

"I'll be back," I told Gerda. "I have some questions of my own."

Gerda nodded.

"His *mother?*" Fiona asked, her voice thick with shock. "His *mother?*"

Aidan, Kyle, Ningul, and Fiona sat around a shaken Gunther in the great room. Ningul and Fiona looked appropriately stunned. Kyle continued to merely watch, fascinated by the twists and turns of the Magical Midway's complicated story.

Aidan looked concerned for the man who had come to be his friend, but nothing on his face demonstrated any surprise at this turn of events.

That was getting a little annoying. My new goal was to do something or say something that would make Aidan look surprised.

Did you know? I asked Samson.

I know what is crucial for me to know as it relates

to you, This was apparently not important for me to understand.

That's convenient.

"That *can't* be my mother," Gunther said flatly. It was as if the level of emotion he felt had overwhelmed him, and the only way to survive the experience was to turn it all off. It was so unlike Gunther that it frightened me. "My mother loved me. My mother *never* would've left me alone if she didn't have to."

"Gunther, I can tell you without a doubt that the ghost Gerda you just met is your mother," Aidan said gently. "Once I meet her perhaps I can tell you more about her past, but reading a ghost can be...tricky. The further we get from life the stranger time runs. I can read within your own timeline that she is who she says she is."

"That cannot be my mother," Gunther disagreed, his voice choked with denial.

A bright light flashed in the room and crack echoed loudly in our ears.

"You made Mama *cry!*" little Anna shrieked as she popped into view. Her normally gentle face screwed up angrily as she stared at Gunther from her perch atop the coffee table. "You're a *mean* person! I don't want a brother like you if you're gonna make Mama cry!"

Gunther stared dispassionately at the furious little girl, and then he sighed.

"Anna, you don't know anything about this, or her—"

"She was *your* mother for ten life years, and she's been *my* mother for twenty ghost years, so I think maybe it's *you* that don't know anything about this, Gunther!" Anna shook her finger at him. "And you would know things if you *let her talk to you*! But, no, you ran off, and told her she wasn't who she was and made her cry! You're a *bad* brother!"

The entire room stared at the family drama unfolding in the sitting area, unsure of precisely what to say, or how to make it better. I took a deep breath and wished that my ringmaster powers had come with a Ph.D. in psychology.

"Anna, Gunther has just had a major shock, and he's having some difficulty processing," I told her. "I know that you love your mom, and you don't want to see her sad, but this is very difficult for everyone. I don't think you yelling at Gunther is going to help."

"I don't care, he deserves it," the little girl stomped her sparkly foot.

Gunther stared at her but said nothing.

"I am so sorry; she disappeared before I could

tell her not to go," Gerda whispered as she phased slowly into view. "We did not mean to intrude. Anna, darling, let's leave Gunther alone, please…"

"No! He made you cry! In my first sisterly act to Gunther, I am going to tell him that he's a bad person, and he shouldn't make you cry," Anna told Gerda, stomping her foot again. "That's what little sisters do, right? Tell big brothers when they are *stupid*? Don't *I* get to do that?"

"Anna, you *already* told me that. Charlotte is right, you don't understand," Gunther told her, taking a deep breath.

"I understand just fine! I'm not stupid, you know! You deserve to be yelled at. You're not talking to Mama! She's been waiting to talk to you for years and years and years! She told me. Well, not until, like, a couple of days ago. Mama tells me things late sometimes. She says I have trouble controlling my…my, um…"

Anna grew quieter and more distracted as she struggled to remember the word.

"You don't keep secrets very well, dear." Gerda held out her hand to help the little girl down off the coffee table. "Gunther has every right to be angry at me, so perhaps you and I should go and let him do that."

"You better hurry up, Gunther," Anna told him

solemnly, stomping over to glare in his face. "I've been waiting five hundred years to have a brother. I'm not gonna wait much more. I can haunt you, you know! *Then* you'll really be sorry!"

"Anna!" Gerda said in the mom-voice every woman seemed to be born with, coupled with the skill to fling it effectively at a misbehaving child.

"Yes, Mama," Anna sighed and dragged her feet as she went back to Gerda. As soon as she grabbed her mother's hand the two of them disappeared.

"That's just *so* amazing," Fiona sighed. Ningul reached for her and cradled her head in his chest to comfort her. Her muffled voice croaked, "I envy you so very much."

"You *envy* me? Are you kidding?" Gunther asked her with surprise. "Have you been paying attention to *anything* that just happened here?"

"I would trade almost *anything in the world* to speak to my mother again," Fiona cried quietly into Ningul's arms. "You have been given a *gift*. Such an *incredible* gift, Gunther. However it may have come about, for whatever reason she did it… I envy you, and I am jealous of you, and I…I…am sad for me," Fiona choked back a sob. "Right now, I am *so* sad for me. I miss my mother so very much."

The sound of Fiona's quiet weeping reached through Gunther's anger, and his face softened.

"I know that you are angry." Ningul gazed over Fiona's head at Gunther. "I would be, too, if I felt as abandoned as you likely did, friend. But my love is right. I lost my mother early. *Many* of us did. It is too often the nature of paranormals in the circus. I suggest you move past your anger quickly so that you can appreciate the gift you have been given."

"We are in a paranormal war, Gunther," Aidan said. "If you take too long to work through this, you may *lose* the chance that you've been given. None of us know at this point what tomorrow will bring."

I glanced at the door to Ms. Elkins area, locked and separate from us still.

Some of us knew what tomorrow would bring.

It surprised me that the future-reading cantankerous old woman and the scary huntress witch who trailed her everywhere had not burst out of their room yet. It wasn't like them not to thrust themselves in the center of our newest drama.

"Thank you all for what you said," Gunther nodded. He reached out for me. "I know that all of you are friends of Charlotte's, but I want you to know that since I've been here, you have all become true friends to me. And I appreciate your words. And I am grateful that you were with me here tonight."

"We actually kinda like you, Gunther," Fiona told him, lifting her tear-stained face to meet his eyes. As she wiped the damp tears from her skin, she half-smiled. "I mean, come on, it's not like Charlotte's got a whole lot of choices for a mate. And even if she did, who would put up with her, ya kin?"

"Hey!" I protested, tugging my hand from Gunther's.

"I only *fake* dated Charlotte, and it could be challenging," Aidan said as Kyle laughed. I glared at him, but he gazed back and winked.

Gunther cracked a smile and recaptured my hand in his with a squeeze.

If my friends could help pull my boyfriend out of the black abyss he had fallen into by making fun of what it was like to date me, that was fine by me.

CHAPTER 3

"You certainly have made life exciting around here, Charlotte," Uncle Phil told me while we walked back to the haunted house. Gunther wasn't ready to face Gerda yet, and I didn't want to go visit the ghost woman alone. I hoped that Uncle Phil (since he was *dead* and all) would have some insight into whatever story she would tell.

"Gerda?" I called down the hallway when my uncle and I entered. A tense stillness had settled over the house, its usual peace heavy with noiseless anticipation. The other ghosts remained out of sight, but I could feel them listening.

"Where is Gunther?" Anna demanded, popping into view.

I jumped.

"Anna, you need to rein it in a little bit," I told her, catching my breath. "Where's your mother?"

"In her room. She's not crying anymore. Thanks to your stupid boyfriend, she probably will again, though. Where *is* he?"

"So now he's *my* stupid boyfriend and not *your* stupid brother?"

Anna moved deeper into the house. Uncle Phil and I followed.

"He's both. And he's stupid either way," the girl mumbled sullenly.

"He's not, though. He surprised, and he's hurt, and he's trying to figure out how he feels, Anna. But he's not stupid," Uncle Phil told the little girl. "For a five-hundred-year-old ghost, you haven't developed a lot of compassion."

"I have *lots* of compassion. For Mama. After all, *she's* the one that lost *everything*," Anna glared at me.

I smiled at her as she led us into the small room that Gerda and Anna called home. The little girl broke into a grin as I winked.

Apparently, even five-hundred-year-old children couldn't stay angry for long.

At the other end of the room, Gunther's mother sat gazing out of the forbidden window in the direction of her long-lost son. Her face seemed glued toward my yurt where a son tried to process his mother's return, but eventually, she pulled her gaze away.

"Gerda," I nodded when she turned to me. She smiled at me and nodded back.

"I suppose you have questions," she said. I nodded.

"One of the first ones is why you never told me who you were." I sat down on a chair in the corner. "You *could* have told me."

"You would've told him." Gunther's mother shook her head. "It was important that no one know that I was here. As I watched you and my son get closer, I knew that your loyalty toward him would make it impossible for you to keep it *from* him. I didn't want to put you in the position of having to make a choice."

"I don't think you know me very well. I haven't told Gunther that you were murdered by the Witches' Council," I pointed out. "I don't go out of my way to hurt Gunther if I can help it."

Gerda stared at me dumbfounded.

"*How* do you know that?"

"Were you?" I asked her without answering her question.

"The Witches' Council wanted to ensure that the thirteenth witch was isolated, alone, I suspect," Gerda said as she sighed. "Despite Gunther being half-human, there were always indications that he would be important to the shift that needed to happen. I suppose Mina felt that murdering me would be the easiest way to damage a young boy. It also ensured that my dear husband would…follow a path in which he was less likely to be a help to Gunther."

"*You* could have changed that, though," I pointed out. "I mean, you're *here*. Your family didn't have to lose you. You could have been there for both your husband and your son. You chose instead to hide here. Why?"

"Mina World cast a spell upon me. Upon my death, I was unable to cross onto the Makepeace Circus grounds or to go to Imperatorial City. My husband rarely leaves the circus grounds, and until my son met you, he was rarely anywhere other than the Makepeace Circus or Imperatorial City."

I knew from the stories that Gunther had told me about growing up that she was probably right. If she genuinely couldn't travel to either place, she would have great difficulty in contacting either of them.

"You could've told *me*, Gerda," Uncle Phil

spoke for the first time. "We would've got word to them."

"That's kind of you to say, Phil. But you would not have." She smiled sadly and shook her head. "The suspicion of the ringmasters for one another is legendary. Or, at least, it has been until your niece became elevated. I had no reason to trust you, and what's more, you had no reason to trust me or Roland."

"We were still both ringmasters," Uncle Phil argued. "What was the worst that would have happened? You *should* have told me, Gerda. We would have worked it out."

"My darker suspicion is that my removal from Gunther was necessary for her ends...if that was the case, the Council being aware that I was here could have caused them to take more drastic action. Like killing Gunther himself," Gerda explained. "So I hid and told no one."

Uncle Phil sat down in the chair next to me and crossed his arms. Though he looked like he was prepared to argue with her, after a few moments, he nodded. "I suppose you're right," he said exhaling. "Sometimes, I forget how it used to be."

"You *are* dead," Gerda smiled. "Time runs

strangely even for you, I am sure. Your body wouldn't change your death." My uncle, who's girlfriend was a djinn, experienced death a little differently than most. As in hardly at all, really, once Jeannie granted his ghost's wish to have a body.

"My body changed my death quite a bit," Uncle Phil agreed.

"Yeah, especially for Jeannie," I mumbled.

"Don't start *that* up again. It's not *my* fault that lady ringmasters get a chastity shield put around them," Uncle Phil said. "I didn't make the rules, you know."

"What's this?" Gerda asked with interest.

"I wasn't even talking about that, Uncle Phil! And I sure as heck wouldn't have brought it up with my boyfriend's mother!"

"You won't need to worry about grandchildren," Uncle Phil told Gerda. "They can't have them, Gunther and Charlotte. Charlotte's ringmaster armor? Doesn't let *anything* through, if you get my drift."

"You and my son can't…?"

"No," I told her, my face flaming red. "No, we can't, and we never will be able to, and this is not a conversation that I want to have. This is between me and Gunther and no one else."

"Come now, Charlotte, we're all family here,"

Uncle Phil scoffed. "There's nothing you can't talk about with your family."

"They can't *what*, Mama?" Anna asked, confused. Gerda patted the little girl's hand and hushed her.

"This is not the topic of conversation we're here to discuss," I said, still blushing hotly. "While I can understand why you didn't visit Gunther and, truthfully, why you didn't get word to him, what I can't understand is why you decided to take up residence here?"

With a smile, Gerda Makepeace told us the story of her death, and I realized Mina World was an irredeemable wretch of a witch.

"It was just another day like any other," Gerda began. Even little Anna sank to the floor, crossing her legs and looking up at her mother. "I think we were in Oregon? Perhaps it was Arizona. In any case, it was a warm summer's day and a perfect day to wander outside the grounds and pick flowers."

Ghosts had a fascinating ability to conjure gossamer hints of what they concentrated on, and as Gerda spoke, the whiff of a flowery sweet scent hit my nose. As she continued looking within herself and reaching back toward her life to tell the tale, more traces of sounds, smells, and visions danced faintly in the little room.

"It was something I enjoyed doing," she smiled. "I always picked flowers for our cabin, different bundles and blossoms that I would place in vases around the place. Roland always insisted that he could blink any number of flowers into existence for me, that I didn't have to pick them individually and do it all by hand, but I was determined."

"Why?" I asked.

"Forgive me for saying so, but ringmasters can become...complacent about their own powers. Things come so very easily to you that you lose the ability to see the beauty in the mundane. Beauty seems commonplace when you can create it out of thin air. I tried to step away from the Makepeace Circus, so I would always remember that I was dazzled by the world before I ever knew magic existed. That the world is magic—even if that magic is much slower and more commonplace. I was determined I would impart that wonder to my son."

Gerda's words *reminded* me of Gunther. The two had the same manner of speaking, a similar way of telling a story and making a point. I had been so surprised by Gunther when we got to know each other because he was *so* unlike his rough and loud father. He seemed more elegant and contemplative, quieter and more gentle.

I realized as Gerda spoke I now knew where that gentleness came from.

"Was Gunther with you?"

Gerda's face darkened. She nodded yes.

"He was nine years old, and he was *such* a happy child. Warm and loving, always willing to give to others no matter what they needed or what he had to sacrifice," Gerda smiled proudly. "Picking flowers was something we did together whenever we could."

The smile dropped from her lips, and her face darkened again.

"We had made our way to a grove of trees, and Gunther had climbed a particularly fantastic one. He was hidden among the great branches and thick leaves when *she* came."

I could see the hint of a great tree in the corner, and my mind's eye saw a young Gunther hiding among the branches, looking out over his mother and the evil that came upon them both on a beautiful summer's afternoon.

My heart broke for them all over again. I knew what was coming.

"There was no run-up, no villain's exposition of why it was happening. She simply appeared. With a raise of her arm, a woman I did not know spat her spell before I was able to take my next breath," Gerda whispered. "Mina World was gone from the clearing before I hit the ground. I never knew whether Gunther saw her, or if my son even knew she was there."

"He's never said anything to me about Mina murdering you, so I don't think he knew," I told her. "Anything's possible—maybe he blocked it out? But if it happened as fast as you say and he was a nine-year-old boy climbing through a tree, my gut tells me that...that he probably just looked down, and you were dead."

Uncle Phil sat silently, horrified.

"I believe that as well," Gerda said and looked up. "I heard Gunther call for me, and when I answered, I realized I had already passed on. I answered back, but he could no longer hear me."

"I don't understand. *We* can see and hear you. So can he, now. Why couldn't he?"

"Human ghosts leave with different abilities, Charlotte," Uncle Phil told me. "Tiffany Drake could likely be seen because that girl was *used* to being the center of attention. Her sheer desire to be noticed and seen gave her the ability to appear to us. The same with her father. Their will was strong, and they didn't want to accept their deaths."

"I realized that I was dead almost instantly, accepted it, and I've always been a *bit* of a shy wallflower," Gerda smiled sadly. "Gunther could not see me, nor could anyone at the Makepeace Circus. The ghosts here at the Magical Midway taught me how to be seen and heard."

"It's also *quite* possible that Mina World worked something into the spell so that you *couldn't* be seen by them," Uncle Phil pointed out. "Since she blocked you from entering the Makepeace Circus or Impy, it *seems* likely she would take other steps to keep you from your family."

"But Gerda overcame that block. I mean, *if* that's what happened," I pointed out to him. Turning to Gerda, I asked, "Did you try to overcome the block from Impy and their circus?"

"Of *course*," Gerda responded. She sounded somewhat offended at my question, and I felt bad for asking it. "At each dark of the moon, when I hoped Mina's magic would be at its weakest. Once, when Gunther attended school in Impy,

Mina even came out to cruelly mock my attempt. It was during that moment I realized who had stolen my life. She taunted me with it."

Gerda closed her eyes, and tiny images of the women standing beyond the wall flickered into focus.

"She told me that I would never be able to overcome her spell, and even if I *could,* it would no longer matter. That without me, my husband had turned into a drunken brute, that my son was a miserable halfling no witch could ever love. That the Makepeace Circus would die with Roland. That she had won."

Mina's spell was so cruel, so brutal that I was shocked, and the taunts made it all the worse. There was something so contemptible about a grown woman so concretely separating a child from his mother, and then *blaming* that mother for the misery her disappearance had wrought. The Witches' Council and its reprehensible behavior turned my stomach.

I wished that Gunther had come with me to hear Gerda's story. I couldn't believe that he would blame his mother after hearing what had been done to them both.

"Was Gunther hurt, Mama?" Anna asked, her sparkly face pale. "Did Mina see him?"

"No, darling child, Mina didn't see Gunther in the trees," Gerda smiled and caressed the child's stricken face. "It happened so fast, and Gunther was very quiet. I don't think she knew that he was there at all, thank goodness."

"He must have been so sad and so scared," she whispered, fat spectral tears rolling down her small face.

"He was," Gerda nodded, her own sparkly eyes growing thick with mist. "He climbed down from the tree and screamed my name, and though I kept trying to answer him, I could not. The poor child…he grabbed my body and worked for two hours dragging it back to the Makepeace Circus. I think he hoped his father could save me."

I winced as I pictured a nine-year-old boy dragging his dead mother through the field of flowers she loved. Gunther's determination, even at that age, was awe-inspiring. My eyes filled with tears and the heartbreaking image.

"Once he…got you back there…"

"As soon as he crossed the border, I moved to follow. The entire Makepeace Circus flickered and blinked out of existence for me." Gerda shuddered. She raised her face and looked somewhat embarrassed. "I think I may have gone quite mad for a time. I didn't know if it was me, or them. If my family was still alive. It was horrible."

"I don't think I can blame you there."

"Is that when I found you, Mama?"

"Yes, my little love." Gerda leaned down and cradled the girl in her lap. "That's when you found me, and you gave me a reason to come back to myself."

"I just cried a lot," she shrugged. "I was alone, and it made me sad. I was so happy when I saw Mama in the field. I didn't want to be alone anymore."

"No one likes to be alone, Anna," I agreed.

"*You* do," she told me. "You stomp into your room by yourself *all the time*."

"Does she now?" Uncle Phil laughed.

"How do *you* know that?"

"Anna, have you been spying on Charlotte?"

"No," the five-hundred-year-old girl of five lied through her adorable little incorporeal teeth. I glared at her, and she smiled widely.

My uncle and I left the haunted house with assurances to Gerda that I would talk to Gunther. I understood his reaction, I really did. The shock at seeing his mother again, the pain he felt that she had abandoned him. Gerda hoped that once he understood what happened and how hard she tried to get back to him that his suffering would be lessened somewhat.

"Please, if he knows *nothing* else," she told Uncle Phil and me as we were leaving, "I want Gunther to know that I never abandoned him. I would have moved heaven and earth to see him, to get to him. I never, ever wanted my son to feel alone. Please, make him understand my weakness was my failure to overcome Mina World's spell. It was not a choice to desert him."

My uncle and I left the haunted house weighted down by the family tragedy we had just heard. We strolled together, meandering through the darkness as if we were on a Sunday afternoon walk. The truth of it was we were only half aware of our surroundings, both of us turning and twisting the story over in our minds. After a few minutes of our slow, lumbering pace, he spoke.

"Your boyfriend is a remarkable man," Uncle Phil said.

"I think so, too," I responded.

"I cannot get over the picture of a nine-year-old boy dragging his mother's body back for help. For two hours. Two hours is an enormous amount of time to a child. But two hours alone, frightened? Two hours of pushing muscles to the limit? At *nine*? The poor child must have been out of his mind that he didn't think to just use magic."

"He may not have known to use it," I told him. "He wasn't sent to Impy for training until after Gerda was killed."

"Surely Roland would have taught him," Uncle Phil said.

"The way you taught me?"

Uncle Phil grew quiet at the reminder of how little actual witch magic he taught me when I first became ringmaster. The ringmaster powers were so strong and so effortless to wield that ringmasters relied on them, seemingly shoving aside the disciplines of ordinary witchcraft they knew in favor of snapping their fingers for everything.

Honestly, I did it, too. It didn't take long to rely on doing things the easy way, and it took no skill to do things the easy way.

It was Gunther who insisted I be trained as a "regular" witch and *his* lessons that made my own inherent powers grow.

"Point taken," Uncle Phil said as we came to my yurt. "In any case, your boyfriend is, truly, a remarkable man."

"Let's hope he's remarkable enough to forgive his mom," I replied.

"Where have you been?" Fortuna asked when we walked in. Fiona and Ningul stood behind her looking concerned.

"Talking to Gerda. Why?"

"Wayland Black showed up here and told Gunther something was wrong with his father," she told me. "They needed him back at the Makepeace Circus. Like, *needed* needed…"

"Like *needed* as in *glowing cats* kind of needed?"

"Glowing cats?" Fortuna asked, confused.

"Samson showed up at my house glowing like a light bulb when Uncle Phil died."

"Nothing was glowing," Fortuna said, confused. "Gunther *did* take Delilah, but she just looked like she always did."

The front door opened and all our eyes turned that direction. Devana walked into the yurt with her head down and her hands clasped in front of her. Despite all of us standing up in the center of the room, she never looked at any of us during her slow, methodical walk. She never spoke to us, and we never talked to her. Our eyes followed her entire route toward Ms. Elkins door.

Opening, entering…at last she turned toward

us and smiled weakly before shutting the barrier back into place.

"Those two are *really* weird," Fiona said.

"Maybe they're just anti-social, love," Ningul said.

"Then why live in a circus? I mean, really now?"

Fortuna continued staring at the closed door, her expression confused.

"What is it?" I asked her.

"I don't know, actually." For a few moments longer, Fortuna stared. Shaking her head, she turned back to us. "Anyway, Gunther left with Wayland, but they ran out of here so fast that I got very little from Wayland's head other than a jumble of panic."

"Why didn't you have Samson get me?"

It just happened, you were in the middle of Gerda's story, and you were just going to move the circus to join it with the Makepeace Circus, anyway.

"You're taking this awfully calmly, Samson. Do you know what's going on? Is it not that important?"

Oh, it's important, Samson thought. *An hour here and there, however, isn't going to change anything that's happening.*

"What do you mean? What's happening?"

"I *truly* hate when they have a conversation, and she speaks out loud," Fiona grumbled to Fortuna. "It's like reading a book where every other page is missing."

"What are you waiting for?" Ethel Elkins screeched, flinging her door open. Devana, pale and shaky, trailed behind her. "Move the circus so we can get on with the funeral!"

"Funeral?" I asked growing pale. "Is Roland going to die?"

"Of course he is," she snapped. "Everyone dies."

"I mean is he dying *right now*?"

"Not *right* now," she said, and I breathed a sigh of relief. "We have to *get* there first. *Then* he can die. Come on, join 'em up. Let's get this death march on the road!"

CHAPTER 4

IN THE MONTHS SINCE I BECAME THE RINGMASTER of the Magical Midway circus, powerful witch extraordinaire, and public enemy number one of the powerful ruling Witches' Council, I'd learned a few things.

One thing I'd learned?

With magic, there's *always* a loophole.

I moved the Magical Midway, all right. I was worried about Roland Makepeace. Heck, I was worried about the entire Makepeace Circus— without Roland, they were defenseless aside from any automatic shielding, and if Roland was hurt deliberately I had no doubt the Witches' Council was behind it. If the Witches' Council was behind it?

Well, I didn't want to think about the second prong of the attack.

So, I did what Ethel Elkins wanted me to do. I moved the Magical Midway, ensuring it was right next to the Makepeace Circus.

Right *next* to the Makepeace Circus.

Not joined with it.

"You have to link them together!" Ethel shouted at me as she followed me out of my yurt.

"I don't," I told her without turning around.

"You do! You do, you do! If you don't join them together, he won't die, and *then* where will we be?" The stout old woman heaved and gasped as she kept up with me while continuing to order me around.

"I'm not doing anything until I find out what's going on over there. You can chase me all the way over into the Makepeace Circus if you want, but I *promise* you, Ethel, nothing's getting done until I decide to do it," I told her. At least I assume I told her. I didn't bother to turn around.

"Did you just call me Ethel?" the old woman shouted, stunned.

"She did at that," Aidan said. He and Kyle came around the big top tent. I waved for them to join us, and they quickly fell in next to me.

"Oh, you again," she complained. "Devana,

can't you balance him to the other side of the world somewhere?"

"That's not allowed, ma'am," Devana answered quietly.

Aidan stopped and whirled on Devana, staring at her sharply. Kyle bumped into me as we all slowed and turned.

"Say nothing!" Ethel Elkins shouted at Aidan. The norn waddled over to him and waved her bejeweled cane in his direction. "You know the rules! Say nothing! You can say nothing! You can't interfere!"

Aidan's face twisted in anger, then fury, then disgust. Kyle put a hand on Aidan's shoulder, but my friend shook it off. Devana stared at him, her eyes clear and her shoulders back. "I know the rules," he told Ms. Elkins, never taking his eyes from Devana. "I wonder if *you* do, old woman."

"She knows everything, and she knows nothing at all," Cama, the death bat, cackled and chittered, flying up on us out of nowhere.

"Aidan, what's the problem?" I asked him.

"I...I...oh, this is maddening!" Aidan shouted in frustration. He balled his fists at his sides and continued staring daggers at the silent, stoic Devana. "Is this all a game to you people? What is *wrong* with you?"

"Your human past has clouded your judgment, Reader," Ethel Elkins responded. She stood between him and Devana. "Say it! Do it, and you'll be out of my hair for good! Go on!"

"Aidan!" I shouted.

"I can't!" Aidan smashed his fist into a barrel along the side of the pathway. Kyle jumped to grab him, but my friend shook off his centaur boyfriend with a violent shove. "She's right. If I tell you, my power will be gone. Forever. The past will be closed to me."

"What? How?"

"Because I can't tell you certain things," Aidan said, pacing with furious rancor. I could feel his bitterness being thrown in all directions like stormy waves. "*She* can't tell you certain things, and *I* can't tell you certain things. And it's not fair, and it's not right, and I am so, so sorry, Charlotte."

"Does she know something? Did she do something? Aidan, come on. Tell me."

"I wish so much that I could," he said through gritted teeth. He threw one last ominous glare at Devana and then turned away.

"Aidan, dude, come on. You're obviously furious about something. Can you tell her *anything*?" Kyle asked him.

"Yeah, there's always a loophole," I told him, laughing bitterly.

"Not this time," Aidan said. He walked up to me and hugged me tightly. "I'm so sorry."

"I don't understand," I told him when he pulled back.

"I know, but you will," Aidan said with certainty. Turning back to the old woman and her silent shadow, he spoke once more. "And when she does? I hope you both have one heck of a head start."

"I stand behind everything I have done," Devana told him defiantly.

"Yeah, *that's* precisely what concerns me," Aidan told her coldly.

Devana's eyes dropped again to the ground.

You have no idea what that was about? I asked Samson as we resumed our walk toward the Makepeace Circus. Aidan and Kyle followed closely behind me, their bodies like a wall between me, Ms. Elkins and Devana.

Our little coven was fracturing even more.

I do not, Samson said. *It is likely that Aidan read something in Devana's past he was uncomfortable with. It is something that, for whatever reason, he is not able to tell you.*

Samson?

Yes?

I had figured all that out for myself.

Then why did you ask me what it was about if you already knew?

I breathed deep and counted to ten, calming myself and trying to dissipate the rising urge to turn around, find the cat, and strangle it until its beady little eyes—

Hey!

Sorry, Samson, I told him. *I was asking if you knew anything beyond the obvious.*

No.

Despite the confusion all these rules produced, I was picking up on the rhythm of all the drama. Samson had become less and less useful the further the prophecy went along. For a while, he claimed he couldn't tell me—eventually, I realized it was that he just didn't *know*.

Samson was my guardian. Mine, and the Magical Midway's. He may be a part of the prophecy, but he wasn't the center. His main concern was me, the Magical Midway, and the people that lived here.

Aidan and Ethel Elkins? They seemed part of

the prophecy. While they stayed on the Magical Midway, they didn't seem particularly interested in it or concerned about the people that called it home. Sometimes, that seemed to include me.

Gunther's concern was the Makepeace Circus. Though he and I were both reluctantly in the middle of this prophecy as well.

And Devana...

I glanced back at the huntress witch to find her still staring at the ground as she walked.

Devana was attached to Ethel Elkins' side like white on rice. They stayed in the same room and rarely chatted with the rest of us except during formal meetings and strategy sessions. We had little social interaction with either of them. I could sense that Devana was, in general, an ethical person. Ethel Elkins, too.

But ethics were a funny thing.

Tiffany Drake had been comfortable with her own narcissistic ethics, too. People that were twisted rarely knew that they were twisted, and to some extent, my power was only as good as someone's self-awareness. If their own ethics were similar to my own, I could read them quite easily. If they were aware their ethics were terrible, at least knowledgeable enough to hide it from people,

I could understand those people quite easily, too.

If their ethics were alien to mine? If they could justify things I never could? Then it became a little more challenging.

We're about to cross, Samson, I told my cat as we came close to the barrier.

I will maintain things here, he responded. *Please remember that sundown is but a few hours away. This is not a good time to be locked out.*

Why do you say that?

I waited for Samson's answer, but it never came.

"Lady Ringmaster!" Ambom called and stomped up to us. "You come with help? You come to help us?"

"Help us?" Wayland Black scoffed, stepping out from behind the gargoyle. "It's more than likely *she's* the reason that Roland's splayed on the floor, you stone-faced ninny."

"Ringmaster not on floor," Ambom told Wayland. His red eyes flared. "Irum move him to bed with pillows, so he sleep good. We not leave ringmaster on floor, Blacksmith."

"Figure of speech, dimwit," Wayland said and rolled his eyes. Wayland Black, the unofficial leader of the carnies at the Makepeace Circus, scanned our little group. His face turned red when he spotted Ethel Elkins and Devana trailing behind. "Before you take another step, Charlotte, get those two out of here. Now."

"Why? I mean, Ethel Elkins technically still has a cabin at this circus. She's from here. What's going on?"

"Butt out, Wayland," the old woman snapped at him.

"Someone should have told you to butt out years ago," he snapped back. "What is *wrong* with you, woman, that you brought a huntress witch with you to this place? Have you no respect at all?"

"Why should Devana not be here?"

"Because the Makepeace Circus doesn't allow huntress witches on their grounds," Aidan told me. "Years ago, a seer told one of Roland's ancestors that a ringmaster would be killed by a huntress witch. Since then, none have been allowed at the Makepeace Circus."

"Well, it's not like she can do *more* damage," I told him. "Wayland, let's worry less about her and more about Roland. What happened?"

"No," he said, and crossed his arms.

"No?"

"That's right. No. Not until the two of them are gone."

A quick sample of Wayland's emotions told me he wasn't demanding this to be ornery. Despite the blacksmith's rough demeanor and combative personality, he was deeply concerned about Roland and Gunther. And he had a deep mistrust at the moment of Ethel and Devana.

"Can the two of you go back to the Magical Midway?" I asked.

"No," Ms. Elkins snapped.

"Jeesh, what is with everyone today?"

"Can you magic her back?"

"Not without joining the circuses," I told him. "And that's not something we want to do just yet. Ms. Elkins claims that once *that* happens, Roland could die."

"He *will* die," she corrected. "And he *needs* to die."

Devana placed a hand on Ethel's arm.

"I *knew* this had something to do with you!" Wayland roared at Devana. The big man barreled across the small clearing, his meaty hands outstretched as he reached toward the delicate woman's throat. Despite his impending attack, she stood calm and defiant.

"You no attack people! Ringmaster says!" Ambom shouted and flung his hand out to block Wayland's advance. The blacksmith bounced against the stony arm and slammed into the dirt on his rear. The gargoyle stood before him and sparked fire from his eyes as he looked down on the angry man. "You behave, Wayland Black! Rules still rules!"

"She's a huntress witch," he told the gargoyle. "The only good huntress witch is a dead huntress witch. If rules are still rules, you walking statue, then get her out!"

"Wait a minute," I told him, holding out my hand to help the large man off the ground. "Ms. Elkins was the one that made a comment, but you went after *Devana*." Wayland Black grasped my hand and stood up, dusting off his already filthy pants. Aidan stepped back and looked away. "Why? Why would you attack her because of what Ethel Elkins said?"

"Because she's a huntress witch!" Wayland's voice dripped with disgust. "If *anyone* could get to a ringmaster, it's one of *her* kind."

I glanced at Devana, but she continued her silent, stoic stare.

"Just join the circuses so we can get on with this!" Ethel Elkins told me, grabbing my arm and shaking it. "Kill the old, in with the new, done and done! You people make this so hard! Just *listen to me,* and we can move this along."

"Did she do something to Roland Makepeace?" I asked the old woman.

Ethel's flapping mouth snapped shut.

"What is it with you people?" I asked them. "Why can't one of you just answer me?"

Wayland stared angrily at the two women. Ethel Elkins leaned on her cane silently, Devana standing behind her breathing steadily, her face red. Aidan remained across from the two, staring. But silent.

"If we were back in Mickwac, Charlotte, I would take these two in for questioning," Kyle told me.

"We haven't even *seen* Roland yet." I said. Kyle and I stepped off to the side.

"I don't *need* to see the unconscious guy to know that those two are hiding something. Repeating aloud over and over that you want someone to die while there are reports that someone tried to murder him is *usually* a good clue to follow," Kyle pointed out.

I looked at the waiting crowd.

"In case you haven't noticed, things are often a *bit* more complicated here."

"I have, actually," Kyle smiled. He glanced back toward the clearing and cast a brief look at each person we brought with us. Including his boyfriend, Aidan. His eyes narrowed slightly as he ran his hand through his chestnut hair. "Everyone has a *justification* for their crime, though, Charlotte. Almost no one thinks 'this is wrong, and there is no reason for it, but I'll do it anyway.' Justification doesn't make it any less wrong."

I stood to the side with Kyle, watching them all.

And then a light bulb went off in my head.

In all this time I had been listening to Ethel Elkins, I just assumed that "our side" was in the right. The Witches' Council was so incredibly wrong in so many different ways we *had* to be the good guys, right? There had to be black and white, good and bad...

...but what if there wasn't?

What if there were no good guys?

Gunther, we're here. How's your dad?

Silence.

Gunther? Can you hear me?

More silence.

"I can't hear Gunther," I called to Aidan. "I'm trying to communicate with him, but I can't get a hold of him."

Aidan's face twisted in confusion. Then shock. Then horror.

"We need to find him," Aidan said. "Now."

"Follow me," Wayland responded without argument and led us briskly toward Roland Makepeace's cabin. The group moved after him with the same speed in a weighted silence that felt so thick I could choke on it.

I reached my feelings out across the Makepeace Circus, psychic tendrils shooting around as I groped for my boyfriend.

My heart felt heavy in my chest as we raced into the cabin and I came face to face with my boyfriend—and realized in the same moment that Gunther, *my* Gunther, was no longer there. His hair was styled in the same way, and his face had the same physical features, but the sneering contempt in his expression contained cruelty I had never seen in him.

A stranger stared back at me from the eyes I knew so well.

An angry stranger.

CHAPTER 5

"Why, hello, *Charlotte*," Gunther smiled. It wasn't the smile I'd grown to love, the one filled with gentle affection. It was a cold smile, a calculating one.

"Who are you?"

"Gunther, of course," he responded with a wave of his hand. "What a silly question."

"Your timeline says otherwise," Aidan said.

"Readers *always* think they know so much," Gunther said, waving his hand again. The lawgiver's ring around his finger was a deep purple-black. "Timelines. As if time is something that can be read like a book."

"Only to those who deserve a view of it."

"You lived as a human," Gunther's voice

cracked like a whip. "No one who lived as a human deserves one ounce of the magic or power that we hold."

"Who's we?" I asked Gunther.

"Oh no, little Charlotte," the person animating my boyfriend's body laughed. "They cannot tell you, and I won't tell you, so where does that leave you?"

"You know who this is?" I asked Aidan.

"I…not entirely, no." He leaned toward me and lowered his voice. "It's not that I'm not allowed to tell you, Charlotte. I don't know. Gunther's energy still remains within his body, and with another energy animating it, the past is knotted in a…strange way. Like the pages of two books that have been shoved together."

"You know, we were *perfectly* fine until you showed up," Wayland growled at me.

"Blacksmith, you should have killed her when you had the chance," Gunther told him, and then he laughed. I felt a flash of murderous rage explode out from my boyfriend, and the energy was so out of the ordinary for Gunther it shocked me. "You were warned."

"What do you mean? What is he…she…it, what is it talking about?" I asked Wayland.

"It doesn't matter. I didn't."

"He was told by a seeress that you would be the cause of the death of Roland Makepeace," Aidan said. "He came upon you once at the Magical Midway when you were younger, and he intended to kill you."

"I should have!" Wayland shouted.

"He didn't. You were only fourteen, and he couldn't bring himself to murder a child in cold blood. Even to keep order."

"I was weak," Wayland whispered.

"Um, thanks for not murdering me," I told him. Gazing up the stairs of the cabin, I turned back to the almost-murdering blacksmith. "Is Roland in his bedroom upstairs?"

"It doesn't matter where he is, you just have to join the two circuses!" Ethel complained and stomped her foot. "You're drawing this out! Just get it over with!"

"The next person that tells me what to do is going to find themselves on the other side of that cabin door." I glared at Ethel.

"With what strength, Ringmaster? You have no god-like power here." Gunther sat down on the couch and leaned back. "Not until you do as the wretched old woman demands and you join the circuses. Then, perhaps, you can take me on."

"Charlotte, we need to go examine Roland

Makepeace," Kyle said, coming forward from the back of the crowd. "This is all dramatic and entertaining, but this entire situation started with Roland."

"No, horse," Gunther told him, laughing. "This entire situation started with *her*."

Oh, Gunther, I thought as I stared at the face I had grown to adore. *If you can hear me, I promise I will get you out of this.*

With Gunther's lawgiver ring black, neither his body or his spirit could hear my promise. Without Samson on the Makepeace Circus fairgrounds, I was alone within my mind. Totally and completely alone.

And I didn't like it.

"How are you staying so calm?" Kyle and I climbed the stairs to the second floor. Aidan stayed downstairs to keep an eye on whoever Gunther contained at the moment, as well as the secrecy twins. My trust in Ms. Elkins and Devana had dropped through the floor. With Ms. Elkins calling for Roland's death, it seemed safer to leave her downstairs. Wayland trailed behind us silently.

Kyle and I peeked into each bedroom, but nothing was disturbed. After two doors, a third revealed Ambom standing alert next to a large bed that contained a terrifyingly still Roland Makepeace. The stony gray gargoyle looked severe and concerned.

With good reason.

Gunther's father was deathly pale, and I barely sensed a heartbeat.

His breathing was shallow, labored. Ambom the gargoyle stood to the right of his ringmaster's bed clutching his hand. Apparently, the gargoyle had some kind of first aid or medic training as he had hooked up an IV to Roland's arm. A variety of magical medical machines beeped. Ambom gazed at the readouts with the intent stare ordinarily visible on the face of any nurse in a human ICU.

"He stable," Ambom tapped against the IV. "Irum and I give water with crystals and watch the machines. He not get better, but he not get worse. He just like this. He be like this since it happened. Well, except he also on ground then."

As soon as we entered, I had tried to heal Gunther's father. My confidence in my ability to help him was deflated when there was no response. No simmering energy, no snap of completeness. Nothing. It was as if I had no power at all.

"This would be so much easier if we could call the Witches' Council for help," I muttered, dropping my hands. Imperatorial City had world class healers, a hospital, all the things we lacked here. I might be able to heal Roland if I brought him over to the Magical Midway, but I didn't know enough about why all this was happening to take that risk. I didn't want to trigger something by moving him off the grounds, something that would kill him. It was possible the Makepeace Circus energy was the only thing keeping him alive.

"For all we know, the Witches Council is behind all this," Kyle pointed out.

I stared at Captain Obvious.

"I know," I told him slowly. "That's *why* I didn't suggest it."

"Oh. Right."

I ran my eyes over Roland at the same time I reached out psychically to confirm that he was actually in there. Considering what was going on with Gunther, I didn't want to make any assumptions. There was fear locked within his body, but little discomfort. As my power's touch reached into the soul of Roland Makepeace, I felt something reach back. Energy clutched and tugged at me, desperately trying to break out.

"He's in there," I told Kyle. "He's frightened, but he's not in any pain."

"Can you tell how he got this way? Magic, an attack, poison?"

I scanned the room but saw no cup or food or anything like when my Uncle Phil was poisoned. Everything looked as it should be. Walking across the room, I peaked in the bathroom and gasped.

"What is it?" Kyle asked.

"It…I…Just come here," I told him, I stared at the wagging tendrils of a black plant growing out of the murky liquid marked "mouthwash." As Kyle stuck his head in behind me, he gasped, too.

"Is that some kind of weird magic mouthwash?"

"I can't imagine anyone would willingly put that stuff in their mouth," I said.

Skinny vines zigged and zagged through the bottle's opening as they searched for…something. Kyle reached out before I could stop him and one vine whipped against his hand with a force I wouldn't have imagined possible from the skinny, tiny plant.

"Darn it, that *really* stings!" Kyle yelped. He brought his finger toward his face.

"Stop!" I screamed, jumping toward him.

At least he had policeman reflexes because, Kyle's bleeding finger stopped just two inches from his open mouth.

"Ringmasters have to ingest a poison to be killed. Don't get that cut anywhere near your mouth—if it can kill a ringmaster, it can no doubt kill you," I told him and held out my hand. "Here, let me try and heal it. Hopefully, I can do at *least* that."

Kyle placed his palm in my hand, and his finger was already starting to swell. Closing my eyes, I pictured the poison within the cut and transmigrated it back to the mouthwash bottle. Then I imagined knitting the small cut back together and sealing his skin. Opening my eyes again, I surveyed my handiwork.

"That's impressive," Kyle smiled. "Where did you learn to do that?"

"Gunther," I told him with a lump in my throat. Tears filled my eyes. "He taught me first aid as soon as I grasped the basics of magic. Considering what's been going on, he thought it would be important. I'm protected, but the people around me..."

"Charlotte, we're going to figure this out,"

Kyle stepped up and hugged me. "We'll get him back in his body, you'll see."

As Kyle captured the angry plant in a plastic bucket to bring down to the others, I bit my lip and nodded.

Better to act confident than admit I wasn't so sure.

"Is that a *death plant*?" Aidan asked, shocked, after Kyle and I returned to the living area. Wayland stayed upstairs with Ambom to watch over Roland.

"There's a death plant?"

"Death comes with many faces," Aidan told Kyle as he leaned forward and squinted. "That plant…you sprinkle the seeds in whatever someone would drink. It's also enspelled to sprout only when it comes into contact with the person that it's targeted to kill."

"Can it only kill the person it's meant for?" I asked him. The tiny plant whipped its vines around in agitation.

"Before it sprouts. Once it's like that, though? It's deadly to anyone."

"It whacked me on my hand," Kyle told Aidan, holding his hand up.

"And yet you're still standing," Gunther said.

"Charlotte was able to heal me."

"Is that so? Well, how *lucky* for you to have found her," Gunther purred. Watching the interplay between whoever was inhabiting Gunther and Kyle, I realized that Gunther's mannerisms were now distinctly feminine. He batted his eyes when he looked up at the handsome detective, coquettishly tilting his head. I reached out and felt the surge of attraction simmering within my boyfriend.

"Freeze," I said to Gunther. He turned and smiled wide.

"Did you think it would be *that* easy?"

Well, no.

But I hoped.

"What was that?" Kyle asked.

"As a lawgiver, the ring gives me certain powers," I told Kyle, holding up my gold ring. "If I say freeze to a guilty party, they should freeze. Gunther didn't, so he must not have been the one to poison his father."

"Unless it only works on the guilty *body*," Kyle pointed out. "Whoever's in there could have done it, but since Gunther didn't, and it's his body, it didn't work."

Aidan winced and looked away.

"I take it you don't know? Well, wait—you don't know, or can't tell me?"

Aidan shook his head. "You're pushing beyond history in some ways, Charlotte. I don't have any reference that I can access for this. I don't know if the lawgiver powers work on a mismatched body and soul. Sorry."

As my mind raced through the situation, Kyle's question as we ascended the stairs came back to me. I was actually somewhat alarmed that I was so calm.

Roland Makepeace was upstairs at death's door because he was slipped a death plant in his mouthwash. Gunther had been taken over by someone, I didn't know who, and I had no idea how to get him back. Ethel Elkins demanded that I join the circuses so Roland Makepeace could move on to the afterlife, which would mean that Gunther would become the ringmaster of—

"You're here because Gunther's father is dying," I said accusingly to Gunther.

"Wow, you *really* are the brainiac everyone says you are," Gunther said dryly. "Why else would I be here? Do you think I hop into bodies to have something to do on a Saturday?"

"Charlotte, none of this matters," Ethel Elkins complained. "Have I steered you wrong yet? I'm telling you, it's time for Roland Makepeace to die. It's just *death*, he won't *mind*. Just join the circuses! You'll find out—"

"I'll find out what? If I'm going to find out anyway, just tell me now."

"She can't, Charlotte," Devana said quietly. The huntress witch looked strained and exhausted.

"Oh, I *can*," Ethel disagreed. Devana winced at the norn's admission. "I just don't *need* to. Nothing would be accomplished by it. Charlotte wouldn't understand, anyway. She doesn't need to understand, she just needs to *do as she's told*. This Gunther thing is not important. It's nothing more than a distraction."

The old woman infuriated me.

"Can you still not see the past of whoever's hanging out in Gunther?" I asked Aidan. His eyes narrowed as Gunther gave him a wide, beaming smile, and then shook his head no. "What is he? Or she, really," I told him. "I think whoever's in there is a woman."

Gunther smiled but said nothing.

"I can't, Charlotte. That mixture of two people is just not…it's not normal. I need clear, linear lines."

"Are you sure that Roland won't die until the circuses are joined together? Is he in any danger at all?"

"Well, he's going to *die*, but that doesn't mean he's in any danger," Ms. Elkins told me, shrugging. "If you would just join the circuses so the man could pop off, you'd see that."

I sat down on the couch and buried my face in my hands.

Standing on Roland's porch by myself, I stared at the sunset. The fiery light crept closer and closer to the horizon. As soon as the sun dipped below it completely, I would be locked out of the Magical Midway overnight, and since I didn't understand why any of this was happening, I didn't know what I risked by missing my travel window.

I didn't want to leave.

"You're handling it better than people who have faced this in the past, if that's any consolation," Aidan said, stepping outside to stand next to me.

"I'd really like to be alone, if you don't mind," I told him without turning from the retreating sun.

"Maybe you would, but you can't be in this, Charlotte." Aidan put his arm around me. "If you try and handle this alone, Charlotte…look, if you try and do it all, you'll fail. Plain and simple."

"Yes, but fail at *what*? What am I even doing, Aidan? I know nothing about the end result or what I'm working toward. All I do know is that everyone around me keeps getting caught in this web of magical warfare, and I don't even know why."

"For what's right," he said quietly.

"That's ambiguous as all get out," I snapped at him and shrugged his arm away.

"Power has solidified over the years," he told me as he stepped back. "The Witches' Council has gathered it up, and it now rests with a few at the very top. Without the ringmasters knowing and without intention, the same thing has happened here. Power, though, Charlotte, is a *finite* resource. If one person hoards it, someone else loses it. You are the only one left who can wrest the power from the Witches' Council."

"For someone to gain tons of it, everybody has to lose it," I murmured.

"Unfortunately, yes."

"From a practical standpoint, it doesn't tell me what's going on or what I should do. I can't heal Roland here, and if I take him from here, I could kill him, anyway."

"Have you really not figured this out yet?"

I turned and stared at Aidan, raising my eyebrow.

"*Nothing* is going to *tell* you what to do, Charlotte. *You* have to figure this out. And then you have to make a choice."

I sighed and turned back toward the setting sun.

"And then I have to live with the consequences."

CHAPTER 6

"I HAVE TO GO," I ANNOUNCED WHEN I WALKED
back in.

"Good, just join the—"

"No," I told Ethel Elkins, cutting her off.
Raising my hand toward the flagellating vines of
death, I set the murderous plant on fire. With a
flash and violent thrashes in the air, it screeched
and then turned to glowing ash.

"That thing *screamed*." Kyle stared in shock at
the pile of black embers.

It did. And it was creepy.

And I couldn't think about it.

"Here's how it's going to go," I told the
assembled group. "I'm heading back to the
Magical Midway. Ambom, Irum, and Wayland

can travel across if something happens and they need to get me. If the worst looks imminent, they can bring Roland across. Since you're so *insistent* that I join the circuses, I suspect that as long as I *don't*, Roland lives."

"You're wasting—"

"*You're* wasting your breath, Ms. Elkins," I cut her off again.

The old woman stared at me. I could feel the frustration flowing off her as she considered my sudden rebellion. What she didn't understand was that I was *tired*. Tired of getting orders I didn't understand, tired of getting demands without an explanation of what the end result would be.

I already didn't trust her. Why *should* I believe her? Her province was the future, and yet a stranger stared back at me from behind Gunther's eyes. Ms. Elkins didn't seem to care at all. She never warned me. Isn't the whole point of having insight into the future to be able to prevent harm? I mean, why else would you even *have* the power?

"What are you going back to the Magical Midway for?" Kyle asked.

"A long night," I told him, frowning as I glanced at Gunther. "I don't know what this is, or why what's happening to Gunther is happening, but I'm not doing anything until I do understand it. And I want to check in with Samson."

At the mention of Samson, Delilah raced out from behind a cupboard and leaped across the room to land on my shoulder. The little kitten's claws dug into my flesh, but with my magical armor, she only managed to shred my shirt. The kitten meowed insistently.

"I have no idea what you're saying, buddy," I told Delilah. She yowled and dove into my front shirt pocket. Popping her head back out, I asked if she wanted to go back with us. With a meow, she dove deeper within the small cloth cavern. "And I'm taking the kitten."

"Now, see here, Charlotte—"

"No, *you* see here, Ms. Elkins." I stepped across the room to confront her. "I've followed your suggestions and demands, and it hasn't kept my friends safe. Right now, I *don't* trust you."

"Hogwash. When in tarnation did I promise you I would keep your friends safe?" Ethel Elkins screeched. "That's not my role!"

"But that's *my* role," I told her. "I took this gig to take care of people. I oppose the Witches' Council because of their willingness to sacrifice people's *lives* to get what they want. I don't know why you thought I would become just like them to *beat* them, but I have news for you—I won't do it."

A slow, steady, insulting golf clap broke the silence.

It was the coldly amused expression on Gunther's face that first made my blood run cold. He sat ramrod straight with his legs crossed. A wry, amused look played across his face while he monotonously clapped. My eyes followed the coal black color of the lawgiver ring as the hands I knew so well moved back and forth.

"It was a *wonderful* speech," Gunther mused as he stopped clapping. "It's *adorable* that you're continuing the fight at all. Futility can be so heroic, though, don't you think?"

"Oh, yeah?" I crossed my arms.

"Yes. Positively adorable."

Gunther leaned forward. I could swear his eyes were glowing with an ominous, dark radiance. After a few minutes, he spoke again.

"You know who wins a war, Ringmaster?"

I stared at Gunther.

"The side that's willing to do anything, sacrifice *anything*, to win it. Your ethics will be the death of all you love, witch."

Those words in Gunther's voice cut me to the quick.

It was all the more painful because as I left the cabin, I wondered if they were right.

Fiona and Anya could barely contain their shock when I related what was happening over at the Makepeace Circus. Ningul sat silently, as usual, taking everything in like a sponge, but every once in a while he glanced back at Ms. Elkins and Devana with concern and suspicion.

"What are we supposed to do now?" Fiona asked. "D'ye kin we can kick whatever is in Gunther right out of 'im?"

"I…do…wait, what?" I asked Fiona as I tried to parse her Scotticism.

"Can we knock whatever's in Gunther out o' 'im?"

"Is your accent actually getting *stronger*?"

"Fiona has been watching *Outlander* on the picture tablet," Ningul told me.

"I canna tell a lie, aye, I have," Fiona nodded and brushed her hair from her eyes.

I stared at her.

"I'll tone it down," she grumbled.

"What she was asking was if there is any way you know of to push whatever is *in* Gunther *out* of him," Ningul explained.

"Not that I know of," I told Ningul. "Maybe if he were here at the Magical Midway I could just will whatever it is out. But whatever's controlling him doesn't strike me as stupid. They have to know I'd try, so my guess is there is no way Gunther's interloper will come here."

"I could just whack him with a stick," Anya said. The tall, fierce woman stood up and pulled out what looked like a nightstick and swung it with a whiz through the air. "A good crack to the skull can dislodge a brain, so it has to be able to whack a spirit out of 'im."

"Anya, that *is* still Gunther's head," I told her with concern. "He's going to need it fully functioning once we fix this."

Anya sat back down on the couch and pulled out a knife.

"No stabbing, either."

"Keep your britches on," she told me as she waved it. "I figured *that* would be the case as soon as you told me I couldn't whack Gunther in the head."

I hadn't seen Anya much the past few months. Frankly, as soon as the prophecy and the relationship with Gunther revved up, all the social dinners and girl time that our group previously enjoyed had kind of dropped by the wayside. Without that, Anya (a naiad) and Avalon (her best friend and the alpha female of the weredeer herd) pretty much avoided the drama as much as they could.

Which meant they avoided me.

Not because Anya disliked drama, mind you. With her shaved head, combat boots, and various weapons hidden around her person, Anya could take any drama head-on (and more than likely gut it like a fish in record time). Avalon, though, was a more gentle soul and had a more delicate disposition. Anya shielded her as much as possible.

Once again, I wondered how the two opposites became so close.

"Drown him?" she asked, cleaning her perfectly manicured fingernails with the hunting knife. "Whoever it is will jump right out of there when they can't breathe."

"Again, it's still *Gunther's* body, Anya. I'd like to hand it back to him intact. Let's just assume we need to accomplish this with all limbs functioning, oxygen animating him, and a beating heart. I'd prefer no bruises, but that's probably negotiable."

"You're taking *all* the fun out of this." Anya pointed her knife at me.

"I don't want to *do* anything just yet," I told her. I got up to put on a kettle for tea. "I called you guys here to help me think through what is happening. If we can figure out who's doing this and why, we just might be able to figure out the least damaging way to undo it all."

"Well, Roland's issue is easy," Uncle Phil said. He walked in and sat down. "Someone clearly wants the Makepeace Circus to pass on to Gunther."

"But Gunther's *not* Gunther." I pulled down the mugs.

"Gunther's not important right now!" Ethel Elkins shouted from her chair.

"He's important to me!" I shouted back while flinging the empty mug across the room toward the old woman. Every person in the room jumped in shock. Every person except Ethel Elkins.

She stared at me like she wanted to kill me.

I had lost the ability to care.

From where I sat, the old woman had let this all happen. She was funny, and sometimes a little crazy, but for the moment in my mind, she was *guilty*. What's more, she was absolutely no help.

Slowly, ominously, the old woman pushed herself up from the chair. Plodding forward without the aid of her golden cane, her steps unfolded toward me as if everything was happening in slow motion. Her white hair came undone and flowed on all sides of her wrinkled face as if the norn's fury was unfurling around her. Ethel's face was now bright red with anger.

"If you ever raise a hand to me again, little girl," Ethel's voice echoed throughout the room, the timbre deepening and layers emerging that I had never heard before, "you will *lose* it before you can blink, ringmaster or no."

"Step back," Aidan said. He stood up and intercepted the unhurried old woman who came toward me with all the focus of a tortoise-like heat-seeking missile. "Whatever insult you have been dealt, norn, it gives you no right to strike her. You are forbidden from harming her."

"I am forbidden from harming *no one*," Ms. Elkins hissed at him.

My heart pounded in my chest. The crazy old woman was…changing, growing, getting bigger and stronger. The potent power coming off her made my ears ring.

Suddenly, she hesitated.

Black goop dripped on her head. Ms. Elkins gnarled hand slowly raised to her wrinkled forehead and gingerly touched the wet dropping. Lifting her gaze, she spotted Cama, the death bat, hanging abnormally. Instead of upside down, the bat was upright on the ceiling, her little claws grasping the beam, her big ears brushing the ceiling...

...and her rear end pointed right at Ethel Elkins.

"You *didn't*!" Ethel Elkins screeched in her old lady voice.

"Gonna cut my bum off for insulting you, old lady?" Cama chittered as she swung her tiny rear around in the air. Still holding on to the rafter, the bat made a big show of targeting her rear like a laser and taking a deep breath...

"Stop! Stop it!" Ms. Elkins screamed at the bat while Devana frantically magicked the sparkly black poo off the old woman. Devana looked horrified, and the rest of us struggled not to laugh. "You're disgusting!"

"I'm why the world has tequila, norn," Cama told her wagging her bum again. "They'd miss *me* a whole lot more than they'd miss *you*."

"The death bat makes tequila?" I whispered to Aidan.

"Bats pollinate blue agave plants," Aidan whispered back.

"Your holiness, you should shower," Devana told the old woman. "There's no way to know what lurks in a death bat's…um…excrement."

"Want some more?" Cama asked, aiming her bum again. "You can examine it! I'll even aim for your eye this time to—"

Ethel Elkins balled her fist toward the bat and shrieked a string of words in a language I didn't know. I assumed from the tone that Ms. Elkins was cursing at the bat, but Cama only laughed and waggled her bum. Once Ms. Elkins exhausted her vocabulary, the old woman shuffled quickly toward her bedroom with Devana close behind.

The door slammed with a resounding bang.

The bat chittered and clicked as she turned back upside down. "That was fun," she squeaked quietly. There was no movement. No words from anyone in the room.

Finally, Kyle cleared his throat.

"Did anyone else know bat poo sparkled?" he asked, looking around. "*I* didn't know bat poo sparkled."

"I eat bugs," Cama told him.

"So?"

"So my poo sparkles from their skeletons," she said. The bat released the ceiling and flew down to hover in front of Kyle. "You should see it when I gorge myself on lightning bugs. It *glows*. Well, for a little while."

"Ew, you eat lightning bugs?"

"Only when I have a date, and I want my guano to be *extra* festive," she answered.

My knocks echoed, but there was no response. Neither Devana or Ms. Elkins called out. Neither appeared.

"I want to talk to you. Alone."

I knocked again, louder.

Silence.

The doorknob wouldn't turn.

"If you don't let me in I'm going to make the door disappear. Then I'm going to walk in and then you're *going* to talk to me."

"Do you have that past reader with you?" Ethel Elkins hollered from inside.

"No, Aidan is still at the table looking up information on body snatching."

The door's lock clicked, and I opened it before the norn could change her mind.

"Wow."

I hadn't been in Ms. Elkins' room since she took it over, moved in, and hardly ever came out, so I had seen none of the changes she had made. The place took my breath away. It was incredible. I couldn't believe I didn't know this was here.

"It makes her holiness feel closer to her roots," Devana explained. She watched me twist my head around and marvel at the ice walls and snow-covered floors. Rustic timber furniture decorated the room, and the pieces were covered in fur blankets and pillows everywhere you looked. In the corner, steam rose from a rock hot tub. "It does get a little chilly in here for me, but it is a lovely environment."

"It *is* beautiful, but I didn't come here to talk about the decoration," I told Devana. I sat down on a chair without being invited.

"Please. Sit down. Pull up a chair, why don't you?" Ms. Elkins crossed her arms and tilted her head. Her tone was wry and sardonic...but it didn't sound angry anymore.

"*Why* do you want me to move the Magical Midway?"

"Because Roland Makepeace has to die."

"I understand *that*," I told her. "I've heard you. Over and over. I understand what you want me to do and the end result you want to see. I need you to tell me *why* you want me to do it. What does Roland's death accomplish? Why do you want him dead?"

"I don't know," Ms. Elkins snapped. "I don't know why things happen in the future, or why things in the present have to happen so the future can be. No one *tells* me these things. And honestly, Charlotte, I don't ask. I don't care. The why of it all doesn't matter."

The old woman waddled toward a tall wooden armoire. She clapped twice, and the clothing on her body changed from her street clothes to a thick cotton muumuu nightgown so fast I didn't even see it happen. "You ask me things like the reasons for them matter. They *don't* matter to me. They matter to you, but if you keep letting them matter to you too much, you're going to *screw this up*."

"Screw *what* up? This is what I mean. You just make these comments like I'm supposed to know what the heck you're talking about. Even now, you're just repeating that it doesn't matter. I don't know if this is a paranormal thing or just a you thing, but I'm tired of it." I was growing angry again.

"I don't care what you're tired of."

"You had better *start* to care, because the less help you are to me the less I'm going bother with you," I told her. Devana helped Ms. Elkins walk from the armoire to the bed. "You're living under my roof, you're living in *my* circus. You may have joined with the circus and bonded to it without my knowledge somehow because of some stupid prophecy, but I can guarantee you, Ms. Elkins, if I need to bar you from this place to protect my family or my friends, I'll do it."

"*Your* circus," Ms. Elkins scoffed. "You still don't understand a thing. You couldn't bar me from this place even if you wanted to."

Ms. Elkins sat down with a plop onto her large fur covered bed. The wood creaked and groaned under her ample weight. Devana gently and reverently helped the old woman shimmy back into the pile of pillows. Once the elderly norn was settled, the huntress witch reached out her hand to Ethel.

"Your holiness, perhaps you should—"

"You are sworn, huntress! Shut your trap!" Somehow, the norn's cane appeared in her hand, and she whacked Devana on her thigh. "There are tales we can't tell! There are things she has to figure out for herself! She must learn! She must *learn*! You know this. Wisdom must be *earned*!"

Devana bowed her head, her eyes closed. Without opening them again, the elegant woman nodded to the old lady and turned away.

"You know, if you disagree with her, you don't have to listen to her," I said to Devana.

"Aye, but I do, Charlotte. *You* don't have to listen to her. *My* oath to her holiness is much different than yours," Devana told me sadly. "I would tell you if I could. Truly, Charlotte, I would tell you if I could. Right now I wish more than anything that I was free to speak."

"You're not free, so *shut your trap*!" Ethel Elkins told her and whacked her again. My eyes narrowed.

"Her holiness is correct. I am not free," Devana told me.

"Yeah, well, you know what, Devana?" I said to her as I got up and walked toward the door. "I'm beginning to wonder if any of us are."

CHAPTER 7

"The books are fascinating," Aidan said as I emerged from the old woman's room.

"The books in your head, or the books on my shelf?"

"He's reading the ones with the words on paper," Fiona told me in a distinctly American accent without looking up from the thick treatise she was studying. "His past reader thing seems to be better for finding out about people."

Aidan, Ningul, and Fiona sat at the table poring over the magic books that Gunther and I had studied so many times before. Kyle paced near the kitchen, his brow knitted together in concentration. On the other side of the room, Anya did the same.

"Quit doing that," I told them both. "You're making me nervous."

"It helps me think," Kyle said and continued his slow pacing. Anya simply ignored me. "Gunther's ring has turned black, and tomorrow as soon as the sun rises, it's going to drop off. That means *you'll* be the only lawgiver left."

"Yeah, it occurred to me. But how do we get it? All show up at dawn and scrambled to grab it as it falls?"

"Don't we have to? I mean, who will pick it up if we don't?" Kyle turned to me. "Never mind, I'll get to that in a minute. The way I see it, there are a bunch of things being accomplished by this little attack."

"Little? You think this is *little*?" Fiona asked.

"Roland Makepeace wouldn't call it little," said Anya as she walked over to us.

"I don't mean…look, it's not a violent, outright confrontation. Not a big clash. We're not all shooting lightning bolts at each other in a field. It's more subtle than that," Kyle frowned. "So, here…what do we know so far? What's happened, and what's been accomplished by what happened? Or what will be? Follow the steps."

"Roland Makepeace was poisoned," I said.

"That would cause the Makepeace Circus to pass to Gunther."

"I still don't see how that helps the Witches' Council," Ningul said.

"Anyone have an idea about that?" Kyle asked.

"It would divide Charlotte and Gunther," Fiona turned. "He'd no longer be able to stay here or spend much time with you at all, really."

"But Gunther *isn't* Gunther," Anya disagreed. "Would it pass to whatever is inside Gunther? How does the power anchor in you, anyway, Charlotte? Is whatever is hiding in him doing it so they can take control of the Makepeace Circus? Is that possible?"

Everyone stared at me and waited. I looked around hopefully for my uncle.

"Where's Uncle Phil?"

"One of the guards came to get him for something," Fiona said. "Something about elephants."

Darn it.

"Well, see it…I mean, it goes…" I trailed off.

I thought back to the first night I became ringmaster and tried to remember when everything snapped into place, and where that snap happened. Where did I feel it? I remembered the darkness, the silence, the bubble, the whirl of energy, but as far as anything specific to how the Magical Midway and I joined?

Nothing.

Finally, I shrugged. "Honestly? I don't know."

A small head popped out of my pocket with a flourish, and tiny paws tapped my mouth. "Meow, Merow...HISSSSSSSSS" Delilah told me as her short hair stood on end.

"What's she saying?" Aidan asked.

"I don't know, she's not my familiar."

The enfant terrible is letting you know that Gunther is still locked within his body, so there are two spirits within. He is not gone, he is just...bound, Samson said as he walked casually through the door.

"Where have *you* been?" I asked him.

The elephants needed help with a mouse.

"For two hours?"

It was a fast mouse. Samson smacked his lips.

Gross.

I relayed what he said to the group.

"If he's still in there, you should be able to communicate with him telepathically, shouldn't you?" Ningul asked.

"Not with the lawgiver ring black," Aidan explained. "Once it turns black, the powers are completely gone, and the person wearing it is deemed—"

He stopped short as he looked at me. His discomfort was clear.

"Unrecoverable," I finished for him, my throat thick with emotions I couldn't even name if I tried. I felt like I was going to throw up. "The magic in the ring has determined that Gunther is unrecoverable."

I closed my eyes as the hopelessness hit me like an ocean wave in a storm.

And your uncle is dead, so clearly things are not set in stone. Magic wants to think it is, but magic is often wrong. You have proven that, Samson shot at me. *Pull yourself together.*

I'm trying.

Try harder, Samson fired back. I opened my eyes.

"Charlotte, we figured all this out before," Fiona said as she grabbed my hand and squeezed. "We don't know how the magic of that ring works, really. This is probably a good thing. Whatever is in Gunther, whatever has taken him over, do we really want it to have even *more* power than it does now?"

"I guess not," I told her.

"We need to figure out how the ringmaster

power passes," Kyle told us, crossing his arms. "Honestly, I don't know how you all have been operating this far without understanding what the heck it is you're dealing with."

"Hey, detective, we've been doing the best we can here," I retorted. My back stiffened. His criticism stung. "I don't know how *you* went through an entire lifetime not realizing you are a centaur, but we all have to deal with these little mysteries, don't we?"

Kyle took a deep breath as if he wanted to argue and then exhaled slowly, nodding. "You're right. I didn't mean to make it sound like you had been negligent. I haven't been here very long, and your point is well taken. I'm sorry."

"Apology accepted."

"Good, now that that's settled." Aidan smiled. "I *do* think Kyle is right. We have two things that we have to deal with right now. One is understanding more about the Magical Midway, and the other is a plan to get that lawgiver ring when it falls off Gunther's hand at dawn. After that, we can deal with Roland and Gunther."

"I can't help you with the ring," Mercy World, a member of the Witches' Council, said quietly from the doorway. "But I think I can help you with the Magical Midway."

The entire room erupted at once.

Ningul grabbed Fiona and thrust her behind him. Crouching over, he brought his hands up defensively ready for a fight. Aidan tilted his head in confusion, no doubt reading Mercy's complicated past. Anya seated herself at the table, her knife placed in front of her, and Kyle gazed at all of us trying to figure out what was going on.

"What are you *doing* here?" I asked her coldly.

"How did you even make it onto the grounds?" Fiona snapped.

"I *am* a member of the Witches' Council," she answered. "We are able to go where we will."

"Ya, that's my *point*," Fiona snapped again.

"I just became aware of the situation with Roland Makepeace," Mercy replied. Her face was tense and worried. She looked tired, almost jaundiced against the bright metallic gold of the Witches' Council robes. "I could not in good conscience stand by while Mina destroyed my best friend's husband as well."

"She broke the agreement with you," Aidan burst out in that annoying past reader way he had. You know, where he exclaimed something, and the rest of us had no clue what the heck he was talking about?

That thing. That was starting to drive me nuts.

"Yes, Reader," Mercy nodded. "Perhaps she believed that after this many years, I would not remember how I came to support her. Or maybe she felt I would no longer care."

"No longer care about what?" I asked.

"She was incorrect," Mercy told Aidan.

"Can someone explain to me what's going on?"I walked across the room to stand by Aidan hoping closer proximity could interject me into their conversation. Or at least impart some understanding.

"She joined the Witches' Council because Mina World promised her that Roland and Gunther would not be harmed if she did. Mina needed someone at her side that was a member of the old family, and Mercy is one of the few left. So, even though Mina killed her friend, she oathed to support Mina's agenda. In exchange for that support, Mina would protect those that Mercy cared about and do them no further harm," Aidan's eyes sparkled. "It is the *only* reason Mercy joined the Council, from what I can tell. To protect Roland and Gunther."

"Oh, I doubt that's the *only* reason," I mumbled.

"The powers of the reader are indeed impressive," Mercy smiled sadly. The small blonde woman remained at the door, waiting. Waiting to be thrown out, waiting to be invited in.

I wasn't ready to do either just yet.

"You joined with a woman that murdered *your best friend*," I observed. "Why would I trust *any* help you offer or *anything* that you have to say?"

"Because I loved Gerda more than I ever loved anyone in this life," Mercy responded, raising her head high. "You, Ringmaster, can search my feelings and know that it's true. Your reader can search my past and know why I have done what I have done. You can judge me for my actions as you will, but for Roland's sake, you must accept my help."

"What you *did* was throw lightning bolts at me the second night we met."

"And *you* shoved *me* back across the expanse to Impy based on suspicion, rumors, innuendo, and nothing," she shot back, a flash of anger coloring her face. "We all do what we need to do to survive in this world."

"I don't trust her." Anya stood up from the

table. Her chair screeched across the floor and fell over as she grabbed the hunting knife. Glancing over at Ningul and Fiona I was surprised to see my friends' hands shaking.

"You trust no one, naiad," Mercy responded. "Your trust is meaningless to me."

"I trust Charlotte," Anya told her and the amazon woman stepped beside me.

"I'm going to ask you again because you still haven't answered my original question, Mercy. *Why* are you here?"

"As I have already said, Mina has broken her oath. In breaking her oath, she has released me from mine," Mercy explained.

"Are you saying that you know for sure that Mina is the one who poisoned Roland Makepeace?" Kyle asked her.

"Mina is currently locked in her palace room and well-guarded. She is unreachable, and has been for the last day or so. When I asked to see her about a Council meeting matter, Mabel explained that she is dealing with the Makepeace Circus," Mercy explained. "Later, I heard about Roland Makepeace's *illness.* I assumed that she had tried to strike him down and I was simply not told about it. For reasons that should be clear. Who else could it possibly be?"

That was the question of the hour.

"And Gunther?" I asked.

Mercy blinked in surprise.

"What *about* young Gunther?" she asked, confused.

"Have you heard anything about what's been done to Gunther?"

"As far as I know, nothing has been…why, has something happened to him as well?"

I glared at the woman. I didn't know what to think.

I knew that Gerda and Mercy had been best friends before Gerda, Gunther's mother, had been struck down by Mina. I had witnessed perplexing flashes and moments of affection from Mercy toward Gunther that I didn't understand at the time. I believed the woman when she said she cared about him.

But she *was* a member of the Witches' Council. And not just some random member.

Her emotional attachment to people from twenty years ago didn't necessarily mean she wasn't evil, and she hadn't done horrible things. It didn't mean she could be trusted now.

Did it?

Mercy was one of three women that held power over the entire paranormal world. It was under her watch that the lawgivers were decimated, that the attack on the Werebears happened. That multiple attacks on us took place.

Mercy was present when the ultimatum was delivered. *Hand over your half-human paranormals,* they demanded. They, the *three* of them, said our half-paranormals didn't deserve to live. The *three* of them. Not two.

Yet...at the time of the confrontation, Mercy seemed shocked when Mina said that Fortuna and Mark, our half-human paranormals, would be killed. She covered it well, her face melting into a mask of contempt for us. Despite that, I saw the horror she tried to conceal. I remembered the pain that flickered across her face and then disappeared, covered by a mask of indifference.

But *was* it a mask?

And then after that confrontation, Gunther said Mercy went to see *Roland.* Delilah told Samson she apologized. The kitten reported that Mercy told Roland there was no longer anything she could do to protect Gunther.

Mercy World and I stared at one another as I worked the past over in my mind.

"You told Roland Makepeace months ago that you could no longer protect Gunther," I said to

Mercy, who continued waiting. "When you and your buddies came to demand our half-humans so you could *slaughter* them."

Mercy winced.

"You apologized to Roland *afterward*, but what would you have done if I hadn't found a solution that got around *your trap*?" I demanded. I stepped up closer to her, my voice rising with each step. "Would you have seen your best friend's son handed over to that miserable woman? For execution? The son *you* supposedly swore to protect?"

Mercy's eyes dropped, and silent tears rolled down her ashen cheeks.

"You've had power for over *twenty years*," I told her. "You mean to tell me that for *twenty years* you committed horrible acts just to protect the two people Gerda loved? Because I have to tell you, lady, if that's the case, you've done a *pretty* crappy job. When they really needed you, you were in a palace while they were poisoned and threatened with death."

To my surprise, Mercy said nothing, her eyes downcast and the tears flowing.

Her sadness didn't move me.

I had been through too much.

"I may not have all the information I need,

Mercy, but I absolutely feel I have enough to know I can't trust *you* as far as I can comfortably spit a wereferret."

"Oh, stop your yammering," Ms. Elkins shouted into the room as her door flew open. "You have to trust her. She's part of all this."

"Lady, I haven't decided if I trust that *you're* part of all this!"

"Oh, whatever," Ethel Elkins waved me away. She waddled in faster than I would have thought her bulk would allow, her muumuu whipping behind her. "When you sling mud, I just make mud pies."

"A huntress witch!" Mercy hissed and she dropped into a combat stance the moment her eyes caught sight of Devana. "How could you allow one of *their kind* under your roof!"

"Tyrant!" Devana hissed back. She crouched down with her hands flat, palms toward Mercy.

"I say we just let them kill each other, m'self," Fiona said quietly.

Ningul nodded, his eyes wide, taking in the two dangerous women poised to strike one another. "My love, I may actually agree with you in this case."

"They won't kill each other," Ms. Elkins said dismissively. "For one, Mercy can't kill a huntress witch. It's forbidden. The Council would banish her. Devana has similar prohibitions going the other way. No one's killing anyone today. I have no death on my calendar. Though Roland Makepeace is now overdue, so scratch that."

"You have a calendar? Of *deaths*?"

"Relax, Ringmaster, you're not on it this year," Ms. Elkins told me.

"Is Gunther?" I asked her.

Devana and Ms. Elkins looked at one another, and the old woman didn't answer.

The group in my room had grown into a crowd. Fiona, Ningul, Anya, Aidan, Kyle and I on one side of the room. Ms. Elkins, Devana, and Mercy World stood on the other side facing each other. Mercy and Devana continued to be on high alert, Ms. Elkins continued to look like none of this really mattered at all.

"Why does *everything* that happens to us always get *exponentially* more complicated?" I asked Aidan. As he opened his mouth to answer me, Ethel Elkins cut him off.

"Because we are in a paradigm shift, young one," the old woman said, but she sounded... different. Her usually crackly, screechy voice deepened in timbre. The lights within the room flashed. Ethel Elkins grew in size, in power, in immensity. The tonality of her words became rich and vibrant. Devana dropped to the floor in supplication in front of her, her head bowed. "The pattern of the world must be reset, and so each action is a lever that leads to other consequences."

Aidan shook as he stared at the glowing woman. Everyone else in the room seemed frozen, awed, gripped in terror at the old woman's constant change. The air in the room grew chilly, the lights continued to lower, and the wrinkled old woman's skin smoothed and began to glow.

"You know, just because you can control the lights and make yourself sparkly doesn't mean I'm suddenly going to drop at your feet like Devana," I told her, crossing my arms. Aidan choked out a warning, but I didn't hear it. Someone's hand grabbed my arm to tug me back, but I shook it off. "*Everyone* can do magic here. You're *not* special."

Charlotte—

Not now, Samson.

But Charlotte—

I said not now, cat.

Ethel Elkins, now much younger, much larger, and much more beautiful, smiled lovingly as Samson fell silent.

"I chose you because of your willful independence, Charlotte Astley of the royal blood," Ethel Elkins told me, her head tilting and her mouth smiling widely. "There are times, however, that it would benefit you to listen to those older and wiser than you more often. It would save you some heartache."

"What, like you? An old woman who's been pulling my strings like a puppet, withholding information? *Right,*" I rolled my eyes.

Charlotte—

Not now, Samson.

"Auntie!" Cama screeched excitedly as she flew in through a window. "Hello, hello, hello Auntie!"

"Greetings, niece, you look well," a youthful, now stunningly beautiful Ethel Elkins smiled at the death bat. Years melted off the woman at the rate of a year a second. "Are you enjoying your stay at my circus?"

"*Your* circus?" I asked Ethel Elkins rudely. It wasn't really a question. It was more like a snide statement of cynicism tinged with a lot of fury and frustration directed toward the arrogant old woman. "How exactly are you under the impression this is *your* circus?"

Charlotte—

Not now, Samson! I've got this!

I don't think you—

"Mama wasn't happy that you didn't come to dinner at the holiday," Cama told Ethel Elkins. My head snapped toward the bat. "You must be super busy lately!"

"As we all are, little one," Ethel Elkins cooed.

Something wasn't making sense.

Cama and Ms. Elkins had been around each other repeatedly. In fact, previous to this moment they had treated each other with obvious contempt. Now, suddenly, they were meeting for holiday dinners?

Charlotte—

Not now, Samson. I'm trying to figure this out. Something weird is going on.

I know, but Charlotte—

"Cama, you called Ethel Elkins 'auntie.' Why?" I asked the bat, ignoring Samson.

"Well, because she *is*," Cama said, zipping around. "I mean, why *else* would I call her that?"

"You never called her that before," I pointed out.

Charlotte—

"Well, she's never been here before, now she *is*," Cama chittered and flew affectionately around the young Ethel Elkins' head. Cama even caressed her hair, and the old woman didn't flinch. She just smiled at me and waited.

Charlotte—

Oh, for goodness sake, what is it, Samson?

I'd like you to meet the Magical Midway. My mistress. And yours.

I stared at Ethel Elkins dumbfounded.

CHAPTER 8

IT TOOK ME ONLY A FEW SECONDS OF MAGICAL probing to realize Ethel Elkins was *gone*.

In place of the curmudgeonly opinionated chubby old lady was a stunningly beautiful, elegant woman with long, flowing platinum white hair, ruby red eyes, and alabaster skin.

"Who *are* you?" I asked her. Devana shook like a leaf as she piously knelt next to the woman. Intense reverence flowed from the huntress witch's position on the floor.

Mercy looked annoyed.

"I *am*," the woman smiled at me.

"She really *is*," Cama chittered and nested more comfortably in the woman's hair.

"Are you…are you a god?"" Fiona whispered.

The invader from the Witches' Council stepped back and leaned against the wall, crossing her arms.

"What is a god, *really*, little one?" the woman smiled widely at Fiona. "Certainly in some circles, I might be considered a goddess. Clearly to the huntress witch I am someone to be worshiped and adored." She tilted her head and flipped her silvery white hair over her shoulder. "We don't concern ourselves with these titles and designations the way that you do. They are unimportant."

"She's not a god," Mercy said flatly.

"Indeed, Mercy is correct, Fiona. Technically, she is not a god," Aidan agreed.

The woman's face flashed anger. She narrowed her red eyes at Aidan, ignoring Mercy. "Whatever you see in the past, reader, doesn't necessarily inform the future. You should be more careful when speaking to those more powerful than *you*."

"I'm not saying you couldn't squash all of us like bugs," Aidan told her casually. "I'm sure you could, in the blink of an eye. In more ways than I could even fathom, even with all my knowledge. I'm just saying, though—you're not a god."

"And what would *you* know the nature of gods?" the woman thundered.

Like, literally.

When she spoke? Outside, I heard thunder rumble.

"Wow, she's even more dramatic than the master told me," Mercy murmured.

"I know everything, really," Aidan told her respectfully. "I have the book of the past contained within me. Now that you and I have met, I can see even *more* of your history. All of it, really. So I know without a doubt that you are no god."

Aidan shrugged.

"Then you must also know I could strike you down where you stand!" she cried. She raised her arms above her head and her hands glowed. The wind whipped around the outside of the yurt, thunder roared, and flashes of lightning illuminated the room as if it were an Austin dance club.

"Yes, I do," my friend nodded, relaxed and unaffected by the display of power. "But I also know you won't."

The woman's hands remained aloft for seconds more as the rest of us stared. Lightning continued to flash, thunder continued to drum, and wind continued to howl for another three, four, and then five seconds. The anger twisted the lovely woman's face into a mask of rage, and I was getting ready to dive under the nearest table for cover when...

Everything stopped. Like, I mean everything. All at once. The woman dropped her hands, silence descended, and calm returned to the room and to the powerful being that had visited us.

"Past-readers are so annoying," the woman murmured as she crossed her arms and glared at Aidan. He smiled. Mercy chuckled.

"Do you wish me to kill him, Mistress?" Devana asked from her prostrated position on the floor at the woman's feet. The huntress witch's voice shook in fear.

"No, I don't wish it at the moment, handmaiden. I may take you up on it at a later time, however."

"Again, *who* the heck are you?" I demanded.

"Aunt Maggie," Cama squeaked.

"Your name is *Maggie*?" It seemed a remarkably normal name for a strikingly abnormal...woman? Shapeshifter? Goddess? I really didn't know what she was, but knowing she was Cama's aunt and the death goddess's sister, I wasn't entirely sure that I bought Aidan's explanation that she *wasn't* a god.

"It means Pearl," she told me as she flung her hair around. The hair had an opalescent shimmer to it. "My parents named me for my lustrous hair."

"Why not just name you Pearl?"

"I would've picked Ruby myself," Fiona observed as the woman narrowed her glowing red eyes at me. "I mean, the hair is not exactly the *most* striking aspect, know what I mean?"

"You are *remarkably* disrespectful considering you wield the power I have entrusted to your family. Yours and the Makepeace family, in any case." Maggie snapped her fingers and manifested a golden throne encrusted with jewels. Settling into it, she leaned forward regally. "Though I must admit I did not choose any of your families for indecisiveness or faltering confidence. So this shouldn't surprise me."

The death bat continued to snuggle happily in the woman's white hair.

"Why are you here?" I asked her.

"I am *always* here in some form, Charlotte." Maggie swept her hand widely, possessively, as if to lay claim to all she beheld. "You have a dome of magic protecting those here because *I* allow it.

You have a cast of armor invisible to all who behold you because *I* will it. You can manifest anything you need, anything you want, anything your heart desires because *I* bestowed upon you the power of a god."

"Oh, for goodness sake," Mercy mumbled and rolled her eyes. "No wonder we're winning. Could she *be* any more full of herself?"

To my surprise, Maggie showed absolutely no reaction to Mercy's impertinence. Instead, the goddess-like woman sat back in her chair looking pleased with herself—as if waiting for me to thank her.

I wasn't quite as snide about what was happening as Mercy, but the arrogance of powerful supernatural beings was no longer something that commanded much reverence in me. I was too frustrated by the forces of destiny that had decided to toy with my life. And this woman? She was claiming she was the reason for *all* of that.

If she wanted a medal, she wasn't going to get it from me.

"Yeah, I get all that. But why are you here?"

Maggie blinked. Her eyes narrowed.

"Do you not wish to thank me for my largess? Are you not pleased to have been elevated to such a position of *power*? Are you not honored to be the very first ringmaster to look upon my true face?" she asked in genuine confusion. "Do you not wish to shower me with accolades?"

"Nope."

Mercy laughed.

The powerful woman seemed stunned. She considered me, her face unreadable.

"*Why* do you not wish to do this?" she asked, genuinely perplexed. "Do you not see the honor that the huntress witch gives me?"

"I see it," I glanced down at the prostrated Devana. "I see it, but I don't understand it."

My assembled group of friends watched the exchange in fascination. I could feel the nerves and fear emanating from different members of the group. All members, in fact, other than Aidan. Even tough cop Kyle was a little concerned about what he witnessed unfolding in front of him.

Samson remained silent, watching. Mercy as well.

"*Clearly* you do not understand who I am," Maggie observed.

I wondered where the superpowered being got *that*. Maybe from my repetitive questions? The ones that she refused to answer?

"Why don't you explain it to me, then?"

"I am the power that animates this place," Maggie began as I sat down. Her face had changed, her expressions became more animated. Her tone switched from arrogant and regal to warm and inviting, like a bardic storyteller that had wandered into a village and was practiced at pulling people in. Yet for the most part, she ignored everyone else in the room and spoke only to me. "I hold the power of transformation. I *am* the power of transformation."

"What do you mean, you *are* the power of transformation?"

"Surely you know how this world and the adjacent ones are governed?"

"Aidan explained a little bit about that," I told her. Samson jumped on my lap. "He said that there were a variety of powerful beings that were in charge of different aspects of humanity and paranity."

"Paranity? What the heck is paranity?" Fiona raised her eyebrow, puzzled.

"You know, humans, paranormals—humanity, paranity. Get it?"

"You just made up a word?"

"I can remake the entire society somehow, but

I can't make up a word? Seriously, *that's* where you draw the line?" I asked her.

"I just don't see what was wrong with calling us all *paranormals*," Fiona mumbled. "Been that way for thousands of years. You just have to go and change it? Okay then. Paranity it is. Even though it sounds silly."

"Nineteen twenty," Aidan said

"Are you counting now?"

"The term paranormal. It's been around for only a hundred years or so. Not thousands."

"You are such a know-it-all!" Fiona rolled her eyes. "And yet we're constantly finding things that you don't know," she snapped and pointed to Maggie. "Explain that, brainiac!"

"What on earth is up with you?" I asked her, surprised by her general level of annoyance all of a sudden.

"Forget it."

Ningul caught my eye and flashed an expression of concern, but he said nothing to Fiona or to me. I made a mental note to try to get him alone later to find out where Fiona's sudden animosity was coming from.

"Whatever you call it," Maggie interjected impatiently, "there are some of us that operate in multiple planes of existence. Though we concern ourselves with the management of your reality, we have access to many levels of them. Including the higher planes that you, as mere mortals, simply cannot access."

"I'm a witch, I'm not mortal."

"You are not *human*, but I assure you, dear Charlotte, you *are* mortal. I've ensured that it is difficult to kill you, but you *can* die. *I* am immortal. *You* are not. This is a *mortal* plane of existence. Everything here is mortal. As mortals, you are guided by immortals. I am one of them."

Great. More rules to learn.

The paranormal world was a certifiable bureaucratic nightmare.

"So you guys are like middle-management?" I asked.

Maggie's smile froze on her still-friendly face. Even so, the frozen smile didn't seem friendly. In fact, there was something downright creepy about it. Mercy burst out laughing at the immortal's reaction. Her ringing peals of laughter, however, did not draw so much as a glance from Maggie.

"Not that there's anything wrong with that," I told her quickly. "Good managers are important."

"Some of us are paired together because our spheres of influence are compatible and must work together," Maggie said as she reached down to caress Devana's hair, ignoring my comment. The huntress witch was still kneeling to the side of the woman, prostrate on the floor. "It is my counterpart that works to tear apart the circus. In concert, obviously, with the Witches' Council."

I glanced at Mercy. She stood, quietly, listening to Maggie.

"Your counterpart?"

"Yes, the other side of my pairing. My partner."

"Is she in contact with Mina? I mean, does Mina know about any of this?"

"He is."

That brought me up short. "He?"

"Yes. My husband would certainly never pass up an opportunity to have a relationship with a powerful, beautiful witch," Maggie spat bitterly. Devana's shaking intensified.

Uh oh. Here we go, Samson thought.

"Eiggam used to be the most wondrous of partners." Maggie stood up and fell again into the musical, expressive tone of storytelling. "He was handsome and powerful…and a wonderful father."

"The two of you have children?" Aidan asked her, confused.

"Of course, silly boy. *You* are our child. Charlotte is our child. Every human, every paranormal, every animal, every living thing on this planet animated by the spark of life is our child."

"So you *are* a goddess!" Fiona exclaimed and her eyes widened.

"Those of you that crawl upon the dirt of the earth are so consumed with that concept, and yet you miss the point. You miss it *all*." Maggie walked around the room slowly. "It's of no matter, dear Fiona; you can call me what you wish. You *may* worship me if you like."

"So you and Eiggam are in charge of all of us?" I asked the easily distracted goddess-like person to bring her back to her story.

"Are you not listening? Eiggam and I are in charge of two aspects of you mortals. I the power of transformation, and Eiggam that power's opposite."

"What's the opposite of transformation?" Kyle asked, looking around the room.

"Stagnation," I told him. "Why would there be a superpowered being in charge of *stagnation?*"

"Stability," Mercy said from the door.

"She's right. 'Stagnation' can be a powerful force, Charlotte," Ningul said quietly from the couch. "There is a permanence to it. Endurance can be a stabilizing force. There can be comfort in inaction, in routine, in dependability."

"Perhaps you should just toddle yourself off to Imperatorial City and join up with my husband, then," Maggie told him, her red eyes sparkling as she crossed her arms and stared down at the quiet centaur.

"Because he understands, you would *banish* him?" Mercy asked Maggie. "Typical."

Maggie did not acknowledge Mercy at all.

"I don't know that I understand what's truly going on here enough to make any decisions, ma'am," Ningul told her respectfully. "It appears that we have been engaged in a fight between you and your husband, assigned to one side, and we were entirely unaware that we were taking part. We were not given the right to choose."

Maggie blinked.

"I would like to hear more. If you don't mind."

Ningul sat back on the couch and waited.

"Is he right?" I asked the mid-level management goddess. "Are we all just pawns in a marital disagreement between two gods?"

"You make this sound so ridiculously silly," Maggie said arrogantly, waving her hands in the air. "Of course, you all are not *pawns* in a marital disagreement between my husband and me. What an absurdly *foolish* thing to say."

"That's good, I'm glad to hear that, at least," I told her. I breathed a sigh of relief. I may be a complete novice at this navigating powerful supernatural beings thing, but the idea that we as people were merely ping-pong balls to be batted around by inappropriately flippant titans in a marital spat over how to raise the kids was enough to make my stomach do flips.

You may want to hold that thought, Samson interjected into my relief.

"You all are the *tools* I've chosen to win the argument against my husband," Maggie explained as she opened her arms wide and looked at us all proudly. "It's everyone *else* in the world, all the *other* mortals, that are the *pawns*."

I expected the room to explode in a cacophony of comments, questions, and exclamations, but it didn't. It was as if Maggie dropped a bomb in the center of the gathering and everyone within the blast radius was struck deaf and dumb by its force.

Did you know about this? I asked Samson.

I knew that Eiggam and Maggie disagreed, and I knew that disagreement led to the withdrawing of their guidance from the world. Their relationship went out of balance, and so they pulled back and concentrated their powers until they could work through it, Samson explained.

You didn't think about telling me this?

Whatever else the mistress is, she is powerful, Charlotte, Samson told me as he rubbed his head against my hand. *I have not been coy with you to make your job harder. I have withheld information from you because I was required to.*

"What does Samson mean, you and Eiggam withdrew your guidance from the world?"

"The world has no stability, and no power of transformation anymore," Maggie explained as she sat back down in her throne. "Those powers have been withdrawn and concentrated in just two places."

"The circuses for transformation, and the Witches' Council for stagnation," I guessed.

"Stability," Mercy called. "Not stagnation, stability. Let's *try* not to be insulting."

"Yes," Maggie nodded. "My circuses were designed to travel all over the world bringing with them the powers of transformation, of dreaming, of joy, of exuberance! No concern for tomorrow, no obsession with yesterday! The sun rises, and we simply do whatever we wish and change however we like!"

"But while the circuses have been flitting around the planet doing whatever they want whenever they want, the Witches' Council has come down like a hammer on paranormals for the last two hundred years. People have been *killed*," I told her, growing angrier. "Your *own* circuses with the traveling power of transformation have been slowly dismantled until there's only two left."

"Well, yes—my husband Eiggam is clearly winning," the goddess shrugged.

"And if he *ultimately* wins, what happens?" I asked her. "What happens to all the paranormals, what happens to the humans? What happens to the world?"

"It will stagnate, Charlotte," Maggie said as she crossed her legs almost girlishly in her throne. The goddess looked even younger than when we started speaking to her. She was shorter, her hair shorter, her face the picture of teenage youth. "I mean, like, what did you *think* was gonna happen?"

"What's going on?" I asked, pointing at Maggie. "Why does she suddenly look sixteen?"

"Oh my gosh, you ask, like, *so* many boring questions," Maggie rolled her eyes. Which were now a brilliant sapphire blue. "The world will be old, and fuddy-duddy, and it will never change. You know what happens when things never change, though? People fight to change them! They beat against the walls, dude. Like, until their fists bleed."

"What the heck is she talking about?"

"May I speak?" Devana whispered.

"Yeah, talk," I told her.

"Oh my gosh, it's not like she was asking *you*," Maggie said rolling her eyes again. She reached out with her small hand and patted Devana's back. "Go ahead, tell them whatever. Maybe *you* can get through to her. I can't believe I picked her. What was I thinking?"

The goddess blew a bubble with gum I didn't even know she had as she continued her transformation into ever-younger youth. If I came across her on the street, I would guess her to be no more than ten.

"What Maggie is attempting to explain to you is that neither constant transformation or constant stagnation is a state that most mortals can exist in permanently," Devana said. She sat back on her feet, still kneeling. "The Witches'

Council is an example of what happens when nothing changes and nothing evolves. People kill one another, scheme against one another, betray one another in a desperate search for the ability to transform themselves and the world around them."

"And constant transformation? What is *our* weakness?" Kyle asked from beside Aidan.

"It is movement without purpose," Devana told him. "Without something stable to stand upon, it is impossible to transform with purpose. People fight to nail down something stable despite the elusiveness of that stability. They create villages that appear as if they never moved, build families to anchor themselves, and then live in constant fear of the impermanence of it all. Transformation has been losing because it is not stable, and one cannot fight without a stable ground to stand on."

"Fearful people don't act any better than people locked in a box, you know," ten-year-old Maggie interjected in between loud snaps of gum.

"Neither side is balanced," Devana concluded. "Each side must engage in a constant fight to achieve that which they cannot, and will live in constant fear because they miss the thing that they cannot find."

"This is all philosophical and highbrow and whatever," I told Devana. I reached down to stand her up. "But what does it mean in *practicality*?"

"What I've explained *is* what it means in practicality, Ringmaster," Devana said as she climbed to her feet. "The Witches' Council can do nothing but enforce an unchangeable stasis. You can do nothing but flit about as if you have nowhere stable to stand. The humans can do nothing but bounce back and forth between retrogression and progression, as if a pendulum swings to and fro with great force rendering their world chaotic. This feeling, this imbalance—this thing between Maggie and Eiggam…it has severe consequences for the nature of the world."

"This is what you were trying to explain to me when you first arrived?" I asked Aidan. He nodded.

"I didn't know the whole of this because, of course, I had not truly met Maggie," Aidan said, nodding toward the five-year-old goddess now curled up on the great golden throne. "But yes, this comports with the story that I explained to you and fits within what I knew at the time."

I turned away from everyone and headed toward the kitchen to boil water for a cup of tea. In all the mystery books I have ever read, many of them with settings in England, a cup of tea was the answer to absolutely everything. Every overwhelming nugget of information, every complex piece of the puzzle…they all required a cup of tea to solve.

"Is Ethel Elkins even still here?" Fiona asked from behind me.

"Maggie is using Ms. Elkins body. Though she has temporarily transformed it to her liking, Ms. Elkins will reappear once Maggie decides to leave us," I heard Devana tell her.

"Maggie's getting bored," the child goddess said. "I think I want to go visit my sisters. Besides, you guys have to go finish killing Roland Makepeace."

I froze for a second in shock at the statement. Whipping around to confront the weirdly changeable goddess, I did not find the five-year-old sitting on the golden throne.

I found only a fat old woman sitting on a wooden chair.

Smirking.

CHAPTER 9

"WHY WOULDN'T IT BE TRUE?" FIONA ASKED ME. Ningul followed behind us.

Rather than get into yet another debate with Ethel Elkins, I did what I always did when I was overwhelmed by the swirling controversy that seemed to rotate around me as if I were the eye of a hurricane. I turned around and walked out the door.

I wasn't running this time, not really.

Time was working against us. Everything that Maggie said swirled through my mind, but even with all of her claims, one overriding concern beat itself in a staccato echoing within my brain. In a few hours, the lawgiver ring would drop off Gunther's hand.

I could only deal with things a step at a time.

As usual, Fiona and Ningul followed me. Aidan and Kyle as well. Ethel Elkins and her dangerous lapdog, the huntress witch Devana, remained in the common room of what used to be my home. So did Mercy despite not being invited to do so.

It's still your home, Samson said.

Home implies a place of solitude, a place of safety, a place of—

Stability? Samson asked.

"Are you telling me that *you're* absolutely sure whatever it is that thing was couldn't possibly be lying to us?" I asked Fiona as we walked toward the edge of the clearing.

"Don't you trust your cat?" Ningul asked. "Witches' familiars are loyal to the witch that they are bonded to, are they not? That relationship is sacrosanct, I thought."

"But Samson *isn't* my familiar, not really," I told Ningul as we walked in the early morning darkness. "He's a guardian, and if it came down to a choice between me and Maggie, I don't think Samson would side with me. Maggie *is* the circus, after all. Or so she claims."

"Isn't his name Sampson?" Aidan asked.

"No, Samson, why?" I called over my shoulder.

"I...no reason, we can talk about it later," Aidan said.

You know, I'm right here. You can just ask me.

I'll ask you questions when I'm ready to deal with the answer. The sun will soon be rising, and right now the lawgiver ring is the most important thing to deal with. It's all I can handle at the moment.

I missed Gunther.

My concern and fear for him aside, I had grown unbelievably used to my boyfriend's observations over the months we were together. Those that followed me through the quietness of the Magical Midway toward the edge of the circus were reliable help in times of trouble. And, honestly, have we had any other times lately? Despite their support, Gunther's absence was something I could feel with every step.

He has become your other half, Samson said.

You've become really talkative all of a sudden, I snapped.

What are you angry at me for?

I didn't bother answering. Samson always claimed to be wise beyond his years. I'm sure if he thought about it all hard enough, he could figure it out.

"Where are we going, anyway?" Fiona asked. We continue to trudge across the dew- covered ground. I was exhausted, and yet adrenaline pumped through my veins pushing me forward.

"Back to the Makepeace Circus."

"Who's going to put the ring on? Assuming, of course, that we can snatch it when it falls off of Gunther's hand," Ningul asked.

"No one, at least not yet," I told him. "I don't want to make any permanent moves until I understand more about what's happening with Roland and Gunther."

We stepped across the small space between the Magical Midway and the Makepeace Circus.

"Back so soon?" Gunther asked when we walked into Roland Makepeace's cabin without knocking. The ring was still black against Gunther's light skin.

"Mina, is that you?" I asked Gunther.

"It took you this long to figure that out?" Gunther sneered.

"What are you and Eiggam up to with this?"

Gunther's mouth gaped open, and all of his facial muscles twitched. After a few moments, his face smoothed back into a mask of indifference. "If I were to explain it to you, it would take all the fun out of it. Color me impressed, though, Charlotte. It only took you a year to figure out what I knew twenty minutes into this."

"Into what?" I asked the being that I was now sure was Mina.

"Oh no," Gunther shook his head. "You need to put your *own* pieces of the puzzle together."

Crossing my arms, I took a deep breath and stared into Gunther's eyes. Gunther returned my gaze evenly, one eyebrow raising in a question I likely wouldn't answer even if he/she asked it.

"Did you poison Roland Makepeace?"

Gunther chuckled.

"Why have you taken over Gunther?"

Gunther stared back.

I knew I had the upper hand here. I just knew it. I just had to figure out *how*.

Maggie. The impetuous goddess's energy permeated both of the circuses left, but for some reason, our powers didn't extend to the other circus's grounds. I could join the carnivals, push them together, and my ringmaster powers *might* reach to the Makepeace Circus, giving me the upper hand.

But doing that would more than likely kill

Roland Makepeace if Ethel Elkins' claims were true. I didn't trust the old woman, but I believed her pronouncement that the joining of the circuses would usher in Roland's death.

So that option was out.

We could physically overcome Gunther, but what would that accomplish? Mina's magic…I mean, if it was Mina in there…

"Darn it," I muttered.

"It's incredibly confusing when you have a mistress that tells you nothing," Gunther responded, his eyes blazing with smug satisfaction. I tried to figure out my next move and my eyes closed as I rummaged through my mind for a solution.

Time ticked away.

"Charlotte!" Gunther shouted. My eyes flew open to see Gunther's body twitching and vibrating on the couch.

No longer was he smug, calm, and relaxed. His hands jerked up and down, right and left, as his body flopped against the furniture. A look of anger flashed across Gunther's face, then one of confusion. Spittle flew from his mouth as Fiona reached for him, her face twisted with sympathy. Ningul held her back.

"What do we *do*?" she asked me over the din of scraping wood against the floor.

"Gunther?" I crept toward him.

"Witness!" Gunther shouted just before his own hand slammed against his mouth hard.

My boyfriend's body settled quickly after that. Gunther spit blood from his mouth, his cheeks crimson with rage. "That hurt more than I care to admit, but at least your idiot boyfriend is back in his box."

"What did he mean, Charlotte?" Fiona asked.

Witness.

My eyes sparked with understanding as I looked down at Gunther.

"I think you've committed a crime," I told Gunther, walking around the table between us. "If you haven't *committed* a crime, I think you've maybe *seen* a crime. Or *know* of a crime."

"What are you talking about?" Gunther asked suspiciously.

"I think that *you* need to submit to questioning," I continued.

Gunther's forehead creased with concern as I walked closer and sat down next to him.

"What do you think you're doing?" Gunther asked, his voice rising with concern.

"My job." I reached out and grabbed his wrist. "Freeze."

Gunther froze.

"Didn't you try that before? You said you tried that before when you were here? But he's a witch," Fiona asked, her face twisted with confusion. The kelpie gaped at the immobile Gunther while I casually sat next to him on the couch. "So is she. This shouldn't be possible. The lawgiver powers don't work on witches. Is it that simple, then? Truly?"

"No," I shook my head. "It's not that simple, but it *is* magic. You can't just say the word, it's about the intent *behind* it. I previously suspected that whatever was in Gunther had poisoned Roland Makepeace, and that's what I thought about when I tried to use the lawgiver powers. Since I was wrong, they didn't work."

"That's what Gunther meant by witness," Ningul said and awe transformed his face. "If you simply wanted to question Gunther as a witness to a crime, and that was your intention, the power would work?"

"Yes, I had questioned a witness at the

Werebear Jamboree, and I was able to freeze him," I explained. "Gunther was reminding me of that. As for him being a witch? I took a chance that if Aidan's power couldn't read what she is, the lawgiver ring wouldn't be able to, either."

"That's *brilliant*, Charlotte," Fiona said. Her face brightened. "And that means Gunther can hear us."

"I'm not sure what good that does, though."

"Well, it means he's alive, at least," Fiona pointed out.

"I never thought otherwise," I told her. Tears shimmered in her eyes. Then she nodded.

Gunther's eyes, meanwhile, were super-wide and they darted around in a panic.

"I guess when you ban a particular type of magic you forget what it can actually do, huh?" I told Gunther-encased Mina. At least, I was pretty sure it was Mina. I guess it was time to find out if I was right.

"What's your name?"

"Mina World," Gunther answered in a strained voice. You could almost hear the witch's attempt to claw back the words. Ningul leaned in, a muscle in his jaw twitching, and watched Gunther closely. Fiona just stared, her face white.

"Why have you taken over Gunther's body?"

"I hoped to be able to take over the Makepeace Circus when Roland Makepeace died," the rough words tore from Gunther's throat.

"How did you know that Roland Makepeace was going to die?"

"My master informed me that Gerda Makepeace had reached out to her son," Gunther responded tightly. "In *our* prophecy, this heralds the beginning of the end for the circuses. When mother and son are reunited, stability will begin to unfurl throughout the land. Our final triumph is near, witch."

"In *your* prophecy?" I asked her.

"Is that a *question*?" Mina spat back.

"Don't we have the same prophecies?"

"What are you, daft?" Mina sneered.

"You must be kidding me," Fiona breathed. "There are two prophecies now, are there?"

"There are *two gods*, moron," Mina snapped at Fiona, Gunther's eyes searching out the surprised kelpie. "If there are two *gods*, there must be two *prophecies*."

"Is there a way for us to avoid…um, whatever dire consequences you think are going to come of Gerda and Gunther meeting again?"

"There was, once," Mina said as she peered into my eyes. "But I made sure that the only person who could avoid the consequences was no longer a part of your party."

"Who would that be?" I asked her.

Suddenly, Gunther's eyes rolled back in his head.

His body vibrated, every limb independently shaking so fast it looked as if Gunther was phasing into another dimension. Fiona, Ningul, and I leaped forward, but we couldn't figure out what to do other than lay hands on Gunther's body to try and still him.

It was as if Gunther was being torn apart from the inside.

It was horrifying.

He vibrated faster, and faster, a low-pitched hum emanating from deep within. My ears felt like I was in an airplane coming in for a landing way too fast. The sound, loud and grinding, made my bones itch.

Suddenly, with a flash, he levitated and dropped back to the couch.

"What just happened?" Fiona yelled over the din of sound that was now…gone. "Oops, sorry. It was loud in here just a minute ago."

I reached out to the unconscious Gunther with my feelings and was relieved to find he was the only one inhabiting his body. "He's back," I told her. I threw myself into his arms and kissed his peaceful face.

Gunther woke up with a start when my ringmaster armor clanged against his lips.

"Ow!" He smiled, lifted his head up and gently wrapped me in his arms. "I appreciate the enthusiasm, but I already smacked myself in the mouth while Mina was camping out. I'm not sure I can take another one."

He seemed relaxed, relieved, and amused. I, on the other hand, felt like all the emotions I had locked up within myself were about to explode my head right the heck off my shoulders.

Gunther's eyes twinkled into mine. Slowly, his face fell as he read my expression. I don't think I even realized I had already fallen apart after throwing myself in his arms, but I had. I could see the sudden alarm in his eyes.

"Hey now, it's okay, Charlotte," Gunther said with concern.Tears shone back from his own eyes. Without my even realizing it, great sobs were tearing free from my body. My hands shook, and my body shivered from the tension I had kept such tight control over snapping free in my relief.

"I'm so sorry," I told Gunther. He moved me next to him and kneeled in front of me. His gentle hands cradled my head while I clutched his wrists. I couldn't let him go.

I hadn't realized how frightened I was, hadn't let myself feel how close I was to losing him, how horrible it was to see his face look at me with anger. "I'm so sorry. I can't believe I'm acting like this. I can't believe I let that happen to you. I'm so sorry."

"You need to stop this," Gunther said gently and gave me a half smile. "You saved me, Charlotte, and you saved my circus. *You* did that."

"I didn't do anything," I sniffed.

"If you hadn't picked up on what I was telling you, you wouldn't have gotten the information out of Mina that you did. Her fear of what else you would drag from her is what *caused* her to leave," Gunther patiently explained. He continued to gently stroke my cheek. "You *did* save me, Charlotte. You did great, hon."

As Gunther pulled his hand away, I saw the ring was again a bright gold.

"How did that happen?" I gasped as I grabbed

his hand. "It was *black*, Gunther. Once it turns black, it's never supposed to turn gold again."

Magic, Gunther thought to me, and then gently kissed me. Pulling back, he searched my eyes with concern. *Can you pull it together? Dad's still in trouble. This isn't over yet.*

I nodded.

CHAPTER 10

Fiona, Ningul, and I tried to catch Gunther up while we climbed the stairs to check on Roland Makepeace. "It was absolutely insane, Gunther," I finished when we reached the second-floor landing. "She shrank down and looked like a child, but you could still feel this insane power emanating from her."

"I couldn't believe that she didn't squash Mercy like a bug," Fiona nodded. "Blondie kept popping off insult after insult to the goddess, and Maggie simply ignored her—"

"Like she wasn't even *there*." I turned to face Fiona. The group stopped behind me just outside Roland Makepeace's bedroom door. Gunther turned around and raised his eyebrow at the group gathered in the narrow hall.

"Yeah, what Charlotte said," Fiona agreed. I nodded and looked at her expectantly. She lifted an eyebrow as I continued to stare at her. "What? That was all I wanted to say."

"Maggie ignored Mercy *as if she wasn't even there*," I repeated to Fiona more emphatically. "Maggie never *looked* at the woman, never acknowledged *anything* she said. Even when she talked about the Witches' Council or her husband Eiggam she *never* said *anything* to Mercy. *At all*."

"I think Charlotte's right," Ningul said, his forehead furrowed. "I don't recall the goddess so much as looking at her."

"What do you think it means?" Fiona asked Ningul. He shrugged, and they both turned back to me. Suddenly little observances, little oddities, shot through my brain and exploded into relevance like fireworks. After a few seconds, I put it together.

"I don't think Maggie even knew that Mercy was in the room." The group stared at me. "Think about it—she shared information that, in the wrong hands, could theoretically be used against us. She exposed weaknesses that we have."

"I don't recall that," Fiona disagreed.

"The first one being that I clearly don't trust her, I don't listen to her," I pointed out. "They'll have to work much harder to defeat us if they think that we're all in lockstep behind Maggie and doing whatever she tells us. Being witnessed during my first contact with Maggie? That's pretty significant, don't you think?"

"Eh, I think you're reaching here," Fiona said. She studied me. "I'm with you on the fact that it's odd Maggie didn't say anything to Mercy. But she's a goddess, Charlotte. She must have a reason for the things that she does—like not taking Mercy's bait."

"Why?"

"Why what?" Fiona asked me.

"*Why* does she have to have a reason for the things that she does? I mean, I'm sure there's a reason for things happening, but why does it have to be a reason that she is in control of? Why does it have to be a conscious reason?"

"Well. Because she's a goddess," Fiona answered, holding up her hands as if it was apparent.

"No, look," I told her. I held up one finger for each fact now running through my brain screaming its significance. "Mercy had no idea that anything had happened to Gunther. That's one. Two, Maggie never seemed to hear or even notice that Mercy was in the room. Three, Maggie never even mentions Gunther, not once, the whole time she was going off on her explanation and history."

"I'm still not following," Fiona said in confusion.

"I don't think the people Eiggam has chosen to work on his behalf can see what's happening, magically, with our people," I told her, slowly putting together the puzzle pieces. "*Think* about it, they *have* to be getting information from their god-thing the same way Maggie's feeding us information through Ms. Elkins. Yet we *never* really get a heads up regarding what Mina, Mabel, and Mercy are going to pull next. We keep getting caught off guard."

"I still think you're reaching," Fiona disagreed. "That's one heck of a leap to make just because it seems like Maggie didn't care about Gunther."

"It's not *just* that," I told her with frustration. "It's that both sides seem to have these huge blind spots…like they have pieces missing that they can't put together. The Witches' Council didn't see that Roland and I could change people into full witches. If they'd *known* that, their *entire* attack about the half-witches and the laws they passed making them illegal would have been *pointless*. That whole exercise was designed to bring us down—yet in the end, all their effort was futile."

"But that's just a fight, Charlotte," Fiona said. "We won. They lost. That's how fights go. Someone has to win, and someone has to lose."

"They are fighting at the direction of a god," I told her. "From what Mercy said, it's clear Eiggam has been communicating with them far longer than Maggie has been with us. So why would he not tell them the attack would fail? I mean, he's a *god*, right? He has to be at least as powerful as Maggie. Wouldn't he *know*?"

"If I follow what you're saying," Gunther said slowly, his eyes flickering with recognition, "you think that Maggie and Eiggam are unable to see what the other side is doing. That they have no insight into the opposition."

"Not just can't see what they're doing," I told him. "Like, *literally* can't see them. At all. You weren't you—Mina was controlling you. She literally had taken up residence inside your body. If I'm right, it's no surprise that Mercy didn't know about what happened to you."

"Because Eiggam couldn't see it," Fiona said, starting to understand.

"Exactly."

"And Maggie didn't know what happened to me because Mina had taken up residence in my body?" Gunther asked.

"Right," I answered. "You were, essentially, a tool of both sides for a short period of time. I don't think either side was concerned with you because both sides—"

"Neither one of them could see me," Gunther finished.

"This is sounding far less like a prophecy and far more like a game," Ningul pointed out. "A game between two mighty beings."

"Two powerful beings that are married and not talking to each other," I added.

"Look, I need to check on my father," Gunther said, his hand still resting on the doorknob. "Mina waylaid me before I even got up the stairs."

"Oh! Right, sorry—I don't think anything's going to happen to him until I join the circuses, though," I told Gunther in an attempt to apologize for ignoring his poisoned, unconscious father on the other side of the door in favor of entertaining a conspiracy theory in the hallway.

No need to apologize, love, Gunther thought as he smiled at me. *We are juggling a lot right now. I know you'd never let anything happen to my father.*

You promised you'd stay out of my head!

You keep saying that. I keep reminding you I did not, Gunther winked.

I sighed to outwardly express a frustration I didn't feel, but I didn't want Gunther to know that. I had missed him just for the few hours he was cut off from me, and I felt safe again.

Though how anyone could feel safe with this confusion wafting around us like mists of doom was beyond me.

"You go out room! You not welcome here!" Ambom shouted at Gunther.

"Ambom, it's really Gunther," I told the angry gargoyle.

The hulking gray monster blinked his red eyes once, then twice. Ningul and Fiona nodded in agreement with me and assured the suspicious guard that Gunther was back.

"I believe for now, but you go to hurt ringmaster, and I have to crush your head," Ambom told Gunther and pointed his long, stony finger at Roland Makepeace's son. "I just want fair warning. In case you are real Gunther.

Welcome back, real Gunther. I hope I not have to crush your head."

"I do, too, Ambom. How's Dad doing?"

"He all same," Ambom told Gunther. His glowing red eyes crinkled as he glanced around the magical machines hooked up to Roland. "He still no get better. He still no get worse. I try all medicines and magics and even gargoyle heal. He just lay there. He not die. He not wake up. He just...that."

That was barely breathing, pale, with a terrifyingly slow heartbeat. I was so glad that Gerda couldn't get onto the Makepeace Circus grounds to see her husband like this. After everything she told me she had been through— losing Gunther, being locked away from her family, trying year after year to get back to them —it was almost a kindness she couldn't witness her husband's peril. I could feel the intense pain in Gunther.

"We know that he was poisoned by a death plant," I told Gunther quietly. He moved a chair next to his father's bed. "Do you know anything about them?"

"Well, they are poisonous, clearly," Gunther said. "As far as I'm aware, there is no antidote or way to keep it from being lethal once it's ingested." Gunther's forehead furrowed as he stared at his father's pale face. "The thing is, though, a death plant is instantaneously lethal. I mean, like, seconds later. My dad shouldn't be lying here in a coma. He should already be dead."

"The probably Gunther is right," Ambom agreed. "Death plant make people super dead super fast. Roland no dead super fast. He almost dead, but not quite dead. Should be, though. Plant is nasty. Plant make dead fast."

"Did you guys not look into this while I was, um—"

"Mina?" Fiona finished for him. Gunther nodded.

"Not really," Fiona said.

"Aidan and I came up here and found the death plant," I told Gunther. "We destroyed it, and I tried to heal him, but I'm not on my circus grounds so I can't."

"Why not just take him back to the Magical Midway?" Gunther asked.

"I don't know what's keeping him alive, Gunther," I pointed out. "If the Makepeace Circus energy is keeping him alive, just taking him off the grounds could kill him."

"So why don't we just join the circuses the

way we did when you turned me into a full witch?"

"Ethel Elkins told Charlotte that would kill him for sure," Ningul told him.

"In fact, Ethel Elkins is demanding that I do just that," I said.

"Even knowing it would kill my father?"

I shifted uncomfortably and nodded.

"It's *more* than that," Fiona told him and shot me an annoyed look. "Ethel Elkins says that your father *has* to die. She's been *demanding* that Charlotte join the circuses since this happened like a broken wereparrot. Her explanation is that we need to get on with killing your father."

"She said *what*? Charlotte?" Gunther gasped. A flush crept up my cheeks and I fought to guard my thoughts so Gunther couldn't see from my own memories just how flippantly Ethel Elkins was speaking of Roland's life.

"I...um...look, she...Fiona's right," I told him. The color drained out of his face. "She won't say why, though, and I'm not gonna do anything until I understand what the heck's going on. I'm not gonna let them kill your father, Gunther."

"Sounds like she's demanding *you* kill my father," Gunther said quietly, pain clouding his features. I was hooked so deeply into Gunther since he had become himself again that I could feel every emotion that raced through him. I expected to feel him recoil from me, and I was stunned when he didn't. What incredible trust he must have for me.

I do, he thought. *I love you. And I know you love me.*

Tears shimmered in my eyes as I gazed at my boyfriend. Clearing my throat, I answered Gunther's last observation loudly and clearly for the room (and most especially, the violent gargoyle that would bust heads to defend his ringmaster against a threat) to hear.

"Well, she is, and I'm not, so that's the end of that."

"Except that he's still in a coma," Fiona pointed out. "We don't know who put him there, or how to get him *out* of it."

"Then we need to figure it out," Gunther said, his jaw tightening.

It was heartbreaking watching Gunther leave his father's bedside. I could see the reluctance in every inch he put between himself and his pale, motionless father as we all moved toward the door. At the last moment, Ambom and Gunther's eyes met. The rough gargoyle grunted with a nod. Gunther nodded back and slowly closed the door on the two men.

"You going to be okay?" I asked him. Ningul and Fiona had raced down the stairs and out the door as soon as we decided to head back to the Magical Midway. For the first time since Gunther had returned to himself, we were alone.

"I feel like I should ask you that question." Gunther's eyes glistened. "You fell apart a little more than I expected down there."

"More than you expected? What, you expect me to handle anything this place throws at me without having one iota of an emotional reaction?" I leaned against the railing. "I'm not a robot, Gunther. I didn't know for sure whether you were still there, whether you would come back. And not for nothing, hearing Mina's cruelty in your voice was…"

"I know, I just…" Gunther tilted his head, stepped forward into my space, and put his hands on my shoulders. "Sometimes you seem so strong, so capable of dealing with anything that's thrown at you that I wonder if you really need me at all."

"Of *course* I need you," I whispered to him, my

eyes blurring with tears. "I don't need you, though, because I *can't* function without you. I need you because I'm a better person and a better ringmaster *with* you in my life. I need you *because* I love you."

Gunther leaned in slowly, carefully, and gently pressed his feathery soft lips against my lips of iron to give me a gentle kiss. It was ironic that I was so strong, so protected, so well defended that not even affection could get through…

"Oh my gosh," I said with a start as I pulled back.

"Well, I'm not really used to *that* kind of reaction from a kiss, but I'll take it," Gunther said. T he corner of his eyes crinkled and amusement.

"No, I just realized I can't…Like, I can't do anything easily that you would normally do in a relationship between a man and a woman," I told him. He pulled back and stared at me. "That was a decision. Don't you understand? Maggie made that decision. That goddess set it up so female ringmasters could *never* have a relationship with a man."

"Hey, now, wait for a second," Gunther scowled. "We *have* a relationship. That may be part of a relationship, but it's not the whole relationship. I'm not any less happy with you because that…that aspect isn't present here."

"No, no, that's *not* what I'm saying," I told him, rolling my eyes. "Maybe I should have used better words. I'm not bringing up criticism of our relationship. I'm just pointing out that for whatever reason, the goddess decided female ringmasters could not be with men."

"I don't know that she realized that's what she was doing at the time, Charlotte," Gunther said after he thought about it. "I think she just wanted to protect the ringmasters and that was a side effect."

"Was it? Really? Was it, though?"

"I don't know," Gunther sighed as he gestured toward the stairs. "It's not something the Makepeace Circus ever had to deal with."

"How come?"

"We never had a female ringmaster," he told me with a shrug. "It wasn't allowed."

"What do you mean, it wasn't *allowed?*"

"I was told that women were not allowed to be ringmasters, so they never had been. There was no story as to why. It was just accepted that men had to be the ringmasters. I mean, why would I question it?" Gunther asked me. "It's right there in the name. Master. That's male. Hey," Gunther said as we crossed the living room toward the door in his father's cabin. "Shouldn't you be a *ringmistress*?"

"I don't know," I shrugged. "Everybody called me ringmaster, so I just figured I was supposed to be called ringmaster."

"I guess since you are one of the only female ones no one ever really worked out a female title for it."

"What do you mean? My uncle told me that the Magical Midway has had female ringmasters before."

"The Magical Midway has, sure, a few," Gunther said, holding open the front door for me. "You are the only circus that has, though. No other circus ever had a female ringmaster. Just you guys."

"Are you kidding me?"

"Nope," Gunther said, closing the door behind him. "Honestly, the Magical Midway has always been known as a bit out there, even for the circus. You guys tended to march to the beat of your own drummer, if you know what I mean."

Gunther and I walked toward the edge of the clearing as the morning sun was turning the sky a beautiful purple-blue. "We need to hurry up," I told him. "If the sun creeps over the horizon before my foot's on the Magical Midway grounds, I'll be locked out of there all day."

"That always struck me as ridiculously weird," Gunther said, speeding up.

"Your dad doesn't have the same issue?"

"No." He placed his hand lightly on my back. "He can come and go whenever he wants. I mean, what would be the point of not being able to get back to the circus? I just figured one of your ancestors did it for some reason I didn't understand."

The light grew brighter, and we both broke into a jog toward the Magical Midway. "I don't know who did it," I panted as we leaped across the small expanse separating the Magical Midway from the Makepeace Circus.

"Made it!" Gunther said when we landed within the Magical Midway.

Little Anna shimmered into view two feet in front of Gunther.

"If I had a foot I would kick you!" Anna fumed.

"Anna, Gunther had a problem—"

"Well, he's got 'nother one," she said crossing her small arms and glaring at her new older brother.

CHAPTER 11

"ANNA, WE'VE GOT A LOT GOING ON RIGHT NOW," I
told her. She stared daggers at Gunther. Gunther,
meanwhile, gazed back at the little ghost girl,
sadness clouding his features. I sensed the
memory of Gerda, her abandonment, and her
return come flooding back. "I know that you
want Gunther to deal with your mom, but his
dad's in trouble and—"

"No, it's okay, Charlotte," my boyfriend broke
in as I tried to shoo away the little ghost. He
sighed with resignation and nodded to Anna.
"After what you told me about my mom and
everything she went through—"

"I didn't tell you anything," I answered,
confused.

"No, but you thought about it a lot while I was with my dad, and I think I got the gist of Mom's story." He continued to gaze down at little Anna. "I think…I think it's time that Mom and I talk."

"You were listening in my head again?"

"You're welcome to listen in mine anytime," Gunther smiled as he waved toward Anna. "I have nothing at all to hide from you, not ever, Charlotte. Come on, Anna, let's go see Mom."

Well, it's not like I had anything *in particular* to hide from Gunther or anything. It was just that… man, a girl needs *some* privacy, you know?

The little girl's face exploded in joy that Gunther's statement acknowledged Gerda's motherhood to both of them. He didn't say *my mom*, and he didn't say *your mom*, and the multi-centenarian five-year-old picked up on the distinct phrasing of calling Gerda plain old *mom*. A quick rummage through Gunther's thoughts demonstrated that the wording was no accident.

"Are you my brother *now*?" she asked excitedly. Her sparkly hands clasped in front of her and she looked up at him both joyous and hopeful.

"I always asked Mom for a little sister," Gunther answered, a shadow passing over his face as the pain stabbed at him. "I think she must

have remembered even after she died. Don't
you?"

"Yep, yes, you bet! Uh huh!" Anna nodded
vigorously. "Come on, come on, Gunther! Come
on, Charlotte! Come on, come on, let's go tell
Mom!"

Anna poofed out of view with a happy pop.

"I think you just made Anna really happy." I
grabbed Gunther's hand and tugged him toward
the haunted house.

"How could you tell?" Gunther joked, but it
wasn't his usual lighthearted banter. The tension
of his father's illness, the reunion with his
mother, and all that I had told him about Maggie
and the circuses was weighing heavily on him. I
could feel him turning over everything in his
mind trying to determine a course of action
for…everything.

"One thing at a time," I told him.

"Are you poking around in my head, Ms.
Astley?"

"You rolled out the red carpet," I responded
without looking at him.

He squeezed my hand, tugging at me to stop. I
turned and raised my eyebrow.

"All my life…well, since my mother passed
away," Gunther said quietly, staring into my eyes.

"I've been alone. At the circus, I was the son of the mean ringmaster whose cruelty could be provoked in an instant, and so people avoided me to avoid provoking him. At school, I was the glowing half-human that didn't belong, and so no kids would befriend me. My head has been a place of isolation for almost as long as I can remember, Charlotte."

"I'm sorry," I told him sincerely. I wasn't sure what else to say.

"Don't be sorry," Gunther shook his head as his mouth curved into a smile. "Understand that for me to not be alone in my head anymore? It's an incredible thing for me. Every time I hear you, every time you acknowledge that you can hear me...well, it reminds me that I'm no longer alone."

I hugged Gunther as gently as I could without, you know, bruising him or breaking any bones. As he gently squeezed back, I caught a glimpse of Devana peeking out of my yurt watching us. Her jaw was clenched, her arms crossed, and as I reached out toward her, I sampled an air of frustration.

"Why do you think that is?" Gunther whispered without releasing me.

"This is going to take some getting used to," I

mumbled. "I don't know, though. Can you see what I'm picking up?"

"I can, but it's pretty non-specific," Gunther answered.

"My power with other people isn't the same as what you and I have," I told him, lowering my mouth against his shoulder, so Devana had no chance of seeing what we were discussing. I didn't know what powers the huntress witch actually had or whether it did any good at all, but it made me feel better.

Fiona walked past Devana and waved to me to come over.

The huntress witch gave one last glance at us and went back inside.

"We're going to see Gerda at the haunted house," I shouted to Fiona down the midway. Fiona leaned forward and cupped her hand to her ear. I repeated it even louder, but she held her hands up and shrugged, waving at me again.

Gunther held his palm upturned and snapped. Suddenly, a white ball of energy centered on his palm. "We are going to speak to my mother first," Gunther said quietly into the white ball. "Is there anything that you need from us right now? If not, we'll be back over as soon as Mom and I get done with our discussion."

With another snap, the white ball zipped over to Fiona and settled in front of her face. "What the heck is that?" I asked Gunther as I watched Fiona interact with the ball.

"A Comball," he said. I nodded as if I had a clue what he was talking about. "It's a simple little spell that brings your words to the other person and takes their words back to you. Things got a bit crazy before we could get to that part of your lessons."

The white ball zipped back to Gunther, and Fiona's voice began talking. "No, everything's fine here, but no one's made any progress with trying to determine who poisoned your Da, Gunther. Everyone still thinks it has to be the Witches' Council. Oh, and Ms. Elkins and Devana are still insistent none of this matters, and you have to get back here to join the circuses. That Witches' Council woman is just standing there saying nothing."

"Has anyone slept yet?" I asked, and the white ball whizzed back to Fiona. A second later it darted back.

"Nope."

"Why don't you guys take a quick nap while Gunther and I talk to his mom?" The white ball whizzed away.

"You know, this works better if you get a bunch of things you want to say and send them," Gunther pointed out as it whizzed back.

"Okay, will do," the ball said in Fiona's voice.

Gunther snapped his fingers one last time, and the ball disappeared.

"What Witches' Council woman?" Gunther asked, and then gasped as he pulled it out of my head. "Mercy World is still *here*? Right now?"

"One thing at a time, Gunther," I told him again.

The whispers sounded like a din of buzzing bees as we walked into the haunted house. I couldn't even remember at this point when humans had last come through the door to be scared, and the house showed that distance from its ultimate purpose. Glowing books littered the shelves where scary skulls had once waited for unsuspecting ticket holders. The darkness that usually permeated the house was gone, banished by bright ghost light orbs lining the hallway.

"Hello?" Gunther called.

The buzzing ceased instantly.

"I know where her room is," I told him,

motioning for him to follow. "It's down here, up the stairs, and to the right."

A fat, scary man popped up in the center of the hallway and glared at me. "You walk in here like you own the place, lady." His fat finger poked through my chest and whooshed out my back. "People live here, you know!"

"I *do* know," I told him, tilting my head to the side. "And, um, I do *kind of* own the place. I'm the ringmaster."

"You are not!" he shouted at me, wiggling his fingers in my face. "There are no girl ringmasters! What kind of game are you pulling here, chick!"

I cleared my throat and my eyes narrowed.

"Bartholomew, is that you?" Gunther asked him, squinting.

"Gunther?" The ghost jumped back into the hallway. "What are you doing here at this circus? Are you running away from the huntress witch, too?"

"I'm—wait, what?"

"I saw that witch sneaking around the Makepeace Circus, and I was like uh uh, no way, no how. I wasn't going to stick around to find out if one of that murderous tart's powers are to make ghosts blink out of existence. No sir, not *this* ghost," the fat man jiggled as he violently shook his head no back and forth. "Did she run *you* off, too? I mean, I wouldn't blame you since you don't have powers to protect yourself and all," he nodded and then gasped, looking shocked. "Are *you* moving to this circus, too?"

"Bart, what are you *talking* about?" Gunther asked him, completely confused.

"Shhhhhhhhhhhh, don't tell the lady ringmaster my real name—wait a minute," Bartholomew flew toward me again. "How is there are lady ringmaster? What is this *strangeness*? Where is *Phil*? Is *she* a huntress witch?" Bartholomew spat out in shock, pointing repeatedly toward me in an ever more agitated attempt to poke me somehow.

"Bart, this is my girlfriend, Charlotte," Gunther told the agitated, panicked ghost calmly. "I can assure you she *is* the ringmaster of the Magical Midway, she's *not* a huntress witch, and Phil *is* still around even though he's a ghost now."

"Is everything all right down here?" Gerda asked as she came around the corner.

"Your son is dating a lady ringmaster!" Bartholomew screamed at Gerda.

"I'm well aware, Bartholomew," Gerda told him wryly.

"There's a lady ringmaster!" he screamed at her again.

"Everyone knows that, Bartholomew," Gerda said. "Charlotte was elevated nearly a year ago."

"Didn't you go to any of the meetings my father had at the circus, Bart?" Gunther asked him—though his eyes cast back and forth at his mother's face.

"Meetings, pfft," Bartholomew rolled his eyes at Gunther. "Ghosts have no need for meetings. One of the benefits of dying is absolutely no meetings."

"Well, if you had, you would have known well in advance of coming here. Speaking of which, *why* are you here, again?"

"I *told* you," Bartholomew said with a shrug. "I ain't staying at a circus when a huntress witch is creeping about. Uh-uh. Not me. No way no how. I didn't stay alive as long as I did by throwing myself in the sights of hunting *anythings,* if you get my meaning."

"Bartholomew showed up here last night and asked if he could stay. I knew you were busy, so we made room for him until you could make a decision, Charlotte," Gerda told me.

"The Magical Midway is suddenly more popular than I would like it to be," I told

Gunther's mother. "Witches' Council witches, norns, ghosts, goddesses…"

"My apologies, Ringmaster." Gerda bowed her head. His mother's genuflecting to me made Gunther bristle a bit. "I felt the decision should be yours. If I should err on the side of banishment in the future, Charlotte, please let me know."

"Oh, for goodness' sake," I rolled my eyes. "Don't banish anyone. I mean, that's kind of extreme and not what I meant…"

"So I can stay?" Bartholomew asked hopefully.

"We don't have huntress witches at the Makepeace Circus, Bart, you know that," Gunther told him shaking his head. "Dad's never allowed it because of what happened to…" Gunther trailed off and looked at his mother.

"Whether Roland allows it or not, I *saw* her with my own two eyes," Bart told Gunther, shaking his head ferociously. His fierce insistence on anything and everything he asserted seemed just another aspect of his personality, and so I didn't pay much attention to the veracity of what he claimed.

But Gunther suddenly looked concerned.

"When was this again?"

"I told you, I *told* you, last *night*," Bartholomew insisted.

"But when last night? Just after the sun went down? The middle of the night? When, exactly?"

"Early, maybe?"

"Was this before or after Dad was poisoned?" Gunther asked the ghost.

"*Your father was poisoned? I knew it! I knew she was up to no good! I knew it! Old Bartholomew may be a pain in the keister, but I know trouble when I see it!*" the ghost shouted. Gerda winced from the sudden volume. Bartholomew blinked and then gaped at Gunther. "What the heck are *you* doing here with your girlfriend, boy? Shouldn't you be with your father?"

"Ambom is with him, and he's stable," Gunther said, his forehead creased. "What did this huntress witch look like, Bart?"

"Beautiful, but they *all* are, right?" the chubby ghost sneered. "Dark hair, dark eyes, light skin. Red robe or gown or something."

Suddenly, I was paying attention to the ghost's rantings. What Bartholomew was describing sounded an awful lot like what Devana was wearing yesterday evening when I came back to the yurt.

Wait—she was coming back to the yurt, too. From where?

"We need to get back to the yurt," I told

Gunther quietly.

"Why? Charlotte, what's wrong?"

I thought back to yesterday evening. My uncle and I were talking about the story we had just heard from Gerda when Fiona walked in with Ningul. She told me that Wayland Black showed up and told Gunther he was needed at the Makepeace Circus, that something had happened to his father. In my mind, I saw myself questioning whether a glowing cat showed up, Fiona answered no…and then we all turned when the front door opened.

Devana walked in with her eyes down, quiet, and walked straight to Ms. Elkins room.

She was wearing a wine-colored gown. Velvet. Her long brown hair was free around her face. Fiona was troubled by Devana's entrance somehow, but couldn't articulate why. I had been so consumed by the story Gerda had told and the news that Roland was ill that it hadn't even occurred to me to sample the state of Devana as she entered.

As we walked to the Makepeace Circus, Aidan had exploded at Ms. Elkins and Devana.

But he couldn't tell me why.

"It's not possible," I told Gunther who had paled reading the images in my mind. "But I don't know what else to think."

"If Mercy from the Witches' Council is hanging around, though, it could be her, too." Gunther lifted an eyebrow. "Maybe Devana was *protecting* my father. Ms. Elkins is supposed to know the future, right? Maybe she saw it coming and sent Devana over there to try and stop it?"

"Mercy? Mercy Lawdottir?" Gerda asked, her eyes shining.

"She's Mercy World now," I told Gerda. "After you passed away, she joined the Witches' Council."

"No, no, that's not *possible*," Gerda shook her head and crinkled her nose. "My Mercy would never have joined the Council. She came to us to get away from all that."

"I can assure you that she's your best friend from when you were alive," I told her quickly, turning back to Gunther, so I didn't have to go down Mercy Lawdottir World's rabbit hole just yet. Not when I didn't know for sure why she was here. "Ethel Elkins has been insistent—"

"A moment, please. My apologies, Charlotte, for interrupting," Gerda said as she moved toward me and reached her ethereal hand out toward my shoulder. "Is my husband all right? You said she was protecting Roland, or she *could* have been. What would she be protecting my husband from? He is a ringmaster and nearly indestructible."

"I…he is…Gunther?" I turned to my boyfriend, unsure of whether to tell Gerda that her husband lay dying in a supposed preordained death that had to happen because of a prophecy. Gunther stared back at me, unsure himself of whether to tell her. In the end, he decided she had a right to know.

"Dad's been poisoned," Gunther told her gently as her face twisted with sadness and concern. "Ambom is watching over him at the Makepeace Circus right now, so for the moment, he's okay. But someone slipped death plant seeds into his mouthwash."

"Death plant seeds!" Gerda's sparkle dimmed in shock.

"That *sounds* like a huntress witch," Bartholomew interjected forcefully.

"Why is his new wife not taking care of him? Is she all right?" Gerda asked. Though her voice was clear and she worked hard to keep the question even, I felt a gut-wrenching sense of anguish from the ghost. Her emotions and concern for Roland were tied in pretzel knots of loss and jealousy.

"Mom," Gunther said after a long silence. "Dad never remarried. He still spends every Saturday night thinking of you."

"Oh, Roland," Gerda sighed even as she winced. Her face contorted as she fought the relief she felt and the guilt that suddenly hammered her. "We promised one another if anything happened to either of us that we wouldn't remain alone, wouldn't pine."

"Yeah, well, Dad remained alone," Gunther smiled even though sadness clouded his features. "And he *definitely* pined. Usually with a bottle of whiskey."

The mother and son stared at one another across the dim hallway, and the gaze seemed weighted by all the lost years. It was like a kaleidoscope of emotions had been unleashed in the tiny corridor as the two worked back through years of pain, yearning, anger, and sadness in moments.

"Your father is in trouble, Gunther," Gerda said and took a deep breath. "This all can wait. Charlotte is right. We need to go back to the yurt."

CHAPTER 12

WHEN I FIRST CAME HERE, MY YURT WAS MY
castle. Okay, it was a tiny castle, a canvas castle. It
was even a dusty castle. The wind blew through it
sometimes, and people walked into it without
knocking whether or not I was curled up in bed
sleeping. As I looked around the great room, a
large gathering place that had replaced my small,
private oasis of solitude, I had to admit my castle
was no longer a castle.

"It's a war room," Gunther told me and the
faces around the room nodded.

"I never wanted to go to war, you know," I
said. Gunther nodded distractedly while he
scanned the faces staring at us. After a few
moments, his eyes narrowed, and he zeroed in on

Mercy World. "She's just been waiting here the whole time?"

"I have," the blonde woman answered, and then paled at a faint scream from the front doorway. I didn't even need to turn around. I knew that Gerda and Mercy were laying eyes upon one another for the first time in nearly twenty years. Gerda had a head's up.

Mercy had none.

Gunther froze and watched.

"It *is* you," Gerda whispered.

"This must be some kind of trick," Mercy said, her face contorted. "You're *dead*. You passed on soon after you died. *No one* could reach you through the spirit board. I tried, repeatedly, and you *never* answered me. *You would have answered me!*"

"Did you ever try outside of the Makepeace Circus or Impy?" I asked her. "Because if you didn't, that might have been your problem. The way it was Gunther's problem for all those years."

"*What* are you talking about?" Mercy asked me.

"Mina killed Gerda and then cast a spell to prevent her from being able to enter the Makepeace Circus or Imperatorial City," I explained to her. "Her ghost couldn't contact her family so long as they were in either place. I suspect that means you couldn't have contacted her if you were *in* either place as well."

"No, that's *not* possible," Mercy whispered, tears bursting from her eyes. "Mina would have told me."

"Are you sure about that?" I asked her.

"It's true, then?" Gerda asked Mercy as she gestured to her golden Witches' Council robes. "You gave in to your family and became the *very* thing you hated? Mercy, *how* could you?"

"Mama, who's the pretty lady?" little Anna whispered. I hadn't realized the small girl had followed us, but she was stuck like glue to her mother's side.

"Not now, Anna," Gerda answered more harshly than I had ever heard her speak. Anna winced and her eyes teared up with sparkle mist.

I held out my hand to her, and the girl raced over to me. Clinging to my hip, I tried to soothe Anna by patting the general area of her ethereal back, but my hand just passed through her.

"It's *not* possible," Mercy whispered again. "This must be a ringmaster's trick."

"Answer me!" Gerda demanded as she stepped forward, fists balled. "How could you join the *very group* that took me away from my family? From my husband, from my son!"

"I joined to *save* your family!" Mercy told her. She turned scarlet with anger. "The Witches' Council has been trying to take down the circuses for hundreds of years! Most have finally gone quietly, giving up and giving in, but Roland *never* would have done so!" Mercy rolled her eyes and glared at me. "Yet it was pointless. Even so, every circus we took down only made Roland and Charlotte stronger!"

"What do you mean?" Gunther asked.

"You are such *ignorant* country rubes," Mercy told Gunther. In her judgmental tone and insulting words I saw the shades of Mina World. "You know nothing of your own history, you know nothing of your own power. Crudely flitting across the world sprinkling pixie dust on the humans—"

"There's no such thing as pixies—" Aidan broke in.

"*It's an expression!*" Mercy raged.

"Everything all right in here?" Bob, the lares guard, poked his head in. "I could hear the ruckus all the way down the west midway path, yo."

"We're fine, Bob," I told him.

"Oh, hey! Dude, that's a Witches' Council

witch," Bob observed as he walked in slowly. "Should I, like…" Bob unsheathed his sword and waved it around, gesticulating wildly in her direction.

"I have no idea how *any* of you people are still alive," Mercy stated flatly as she stared at Bob.

"Well, I'm *not*," Gerda told her angrily.

Mercy winced.

"They're alive because of me," Ms. Elkins said as she exited her bedroom. Devana trailed behind her as always.

"Yeah, I don't know if I'd go *that* far," I told Mercy, disagreeing with Ethel Elkins.

"Can it, Ringmaster, no one asked you," Ms. Elkins snapped at me. "You *just* found out that you were under Maggie's control, so you're not *exactly* the fount of wisdom here, are you?"

The room erupted in recriminations and verbal attacks. Fiona jumped out of her seat and shook her finger at Ms. Elkins while demanding she show me some respect. Mercy and Gerda moved closer to one another and argued over the course of Mercy's life since Gerda's untimely murder. Gunther stepped up to Mercy, warning her to back away from his mother. Bob's head bounced back and forth in a desperate attempt to spot the first fight that would come to blows so he could stop it.

Little Anna scrunched her eyes shut and clung harder to my leg. So hard, in fact, that it grew icy cold and numb from the spirit's energy.

"Enough!" I shouted in frustration. "Are you people insane? Roland Makepeace is lying on his deathbed at the Makepeace Circus, and we *still* don't know who tried to kill him, or how to save him—"

"I know who tried to kill him," Mercy said with a shrug and pointed toward Ms. Elkins and Devana. "That huntress witch. She's dragging all that guilt around with her like they were gigantic boulders. She's practically wearing a psychic sign over her head that says 'I did it.' Are you telling me not *one* of you supposed witches picked up on that?"

Every head in the room snapped to stare at Devana in shock.

Every head but Ms. Elkins'.

"She's a member of the Witches' Council," Fiona told me as we stared at Devana. The huntress witch's eyes were downcast, her hair falling demurely over her features to hide her face. "I wouldn't believe someone in gold robes if they told me the sky was blue."

"You know, ironically, the earth's sky is violet, not blue," Aidan said to Fiona. Kyle jumped to grab him before he could continue his wholly inappropriate observation. "We only see it as blue because—"

"Hey, walking encyclopedia of every fact in the world?" Fiona pointed at him. "I don't care."

"Right." Aidan stepped back with Kyle. "Sorry, I just—"

"Stop talking," Fiona snapped.

"I have no reason to lie," Mercy said, still eying Gerda.

"You have no reason to be truthful," Gerda told her.

"Did you?" I burst out before anyone else could argue about who was or wasn't telling the truth.

"Did I what?" Gerda asked, confused.

"Not you," I told Gunther's mother. I moved toward Ms. Elkins and Devana. "Her. Devana. Was it you?" I asked the huntress witch. "Look at me, Devana. Have we been running around like chickens with our heads cut off trying to figure out what's going on when it was you *all along*?"

Silence.

"No pronouncement about how chickens don't run around after their heads are cut off?" Fiona asked Aidan.

"Oh, no, they actually do," Aidan's eyes widened. "In fact, there was a chicken named Mike that lived for eighteen months without a—"

"Yes," Devana said. She raised her head defiantly. The woman's gaze was clear, her face steady. "I poisoned Roland Makepeace. It was for the greater good. His death must take place, and I hastened it."

"Was it not enough for my son to lose his mother at the hands of the Witches' Council?" Gerda asked her angrily. "Are the circuses determined to take his *father* from him now, too?"

Devana did not respond.

"This is *your* doing." I held up a hand to Gerda and approached Ethel Elkins. "Devana follows you around like a slave. She would never raise a finger against anyone. Not unless you told her to."

"Ms. Elkins?" Gerda asked, shaking her head. "That sweet old woman wouldn't hurt a fly. I don't believe it."

"Sweet old woman?" I asked, incredulous.

Ethel Elkins sighed. "Gerda, we were trying to

help you. Well," the old woman tilted her head, "among *other* things, we were trying to help you. The other things were significant, mind you. But you would have got quite a lot out of the deal, too."

"Freeze!" I shouted, extending my hands toward the two women.

They froze.

And they didn't freeze because of some loophole in the lawgiver ring that let me freeze a norn and a witch.

This was *my* circus. And I was *still* the ringmaster.

Here, I had the power.

Regardless of what anyone else thought.

And boy, did I sense that Ethel Elkins was *surprised*.

The women's eyes bounced around from face to face, but their eyes couldn't widen and their mouths no longer moved. If pupils could be considered expressive, though, their glassy stares were surprised, accusatory, and furious.

Maybe that was just what I was sensing from Ethel Elkins.

"I know you can both hear me," I said when their eyes fixed on me. "I welcomed you into my circus. I listened to what you had to say. I tried to understand your viewpoints. I gave you beds under my roof. I put up with your demands that I *kill my boyfriend's father*! But I'm...I'm done. You are both guilty of attempted murder. I don't care who was the mastermind and who was the hand. You're both guilty."

"Charlotte—"

"Gunther," I said quietly as he tried to interrupt me. "Don't. Not now. Just don't."

His brows knitted together and I heard one more *Charlotte* echo in my mind before he stopped himself. Then Gunther nodded.

"Bob," I said turning to the lares guard. "Get your brothers and take these two into the security building jail."

Bob nodded and started to walk out the door. Then he skidded to a stop, turned, and raised his hand. With an eye roll, I gestured for him to spit it out.

"Um...we don't have a jail in there," Bob pointed out. "We used the centaur building with Alexa. Should I take them there?"

I closed my eyes and reopened them just a second later. "You do now."

"Sure thing, boss," Bob nodded.

"I don't want them hurt," I told him as he

turned. "I just want them…out of the way for the moment."

"Shouldn't we question them?" Fiona asked me. Ningul nodded.

"Wow, this really *is* amateur hour," Mercy murmured.

"I'm getting to you," I told Mercy and walked out the door to find Fortuna Delphi.

"Come in," Fortuna called. I pushed into her small yurt to find our newest witch lying on her bed with what looked like a washcloth over her eyes. "Please leave the lights off, if you could, Charlotte."

"Are you all right?"

"I've had a terrible headache for about a day now," she answered across the darkness of her small room. Fortuna's voice was raspy, and she sounded exhausted. "It kind of hit me out of nowhere. This afternoon it got so bad, I couldn't look at the words on the page anymore. I felt terrible, but I was useless to Fiona and Aidan."

"They had Kyle and Ningul to help out." I sat down gently on her bed. "Want me to try and heal it?"

"Would you?" she asked gratefully. "Sometimes I wish Mark had chosen to become a witch instead of a lion shifter. When you and Gunther are gone, there are few with healing powers."

"Didn't try and ask Devana?" I hovered my hands slightly over her own.

"I might have, but every time I got closer to her, the headache grew more and more pronounced."

I wasn't surprised.

My hands grew warm, and a glow encased Fortuna's face. I used the ringmaster powers instead of my own magical powers. The first reason was just that they were faster, stronger. The second reason was that...well, because I just froze and imprisoned Maggie's two lapdogs, I wasn't all that sure I would have ringmaster powers anymore. This seemed an excellent way to check.

It was a great relief to me that I felt a great relief from Fortuna.

"That's incredible," Fortuna sighed as she snapped her fingers and the lights flared. "I tried everything, and nothing helped. Magic, potions, human solutions of quiet and a cool cloth. No matter what I did, it just kept getting worse."

"Well, that's probably because someone had put a clamp on your head," I told her. "At least, I'm *guessing* that."

"A clamp on my head? What do you mean?" Fortuna sat up cross-legged on her bed.

The quiet psychic listened while I caught her up on all the things that had taken place since she had fallen asleep. Fortuna's face was impassive. I outlined what had taken place at the Makepeace Circus, but she looked saddened by the situation between Gerda and Gunther, shocked at the Witches' Council shenanigans, and horrified by Devana's admission that she was the one who poisoned Roland.

"I have Ethel Elkins and Devana in jail—"

"In the centaur village?"

"No, I put one in the security building," I told her. "I was coming to get you to see if you could help me out when I question Mercy. She claims she's here because Mina broke her word and harmed Roland, but when it became clear that Devana was the one that tried to kill him? Well, she didn't leave."

"You want to know what her deal is," Fortuna said.

"I want a powerful telepath to tell me what's really going on in her mind," I nodded. "I can see snippets of things, flashes, feelings, but you're much more powerful than me. Telepathy is not a ringmaster power. *You* can rummage around in people's minds and pluck out what they don't want to see. Sometimes, what they don't even know is there."

Fortuna nodded.

"So, will you help me?"

"Of course, Charlotte," she smiled at me warmly, pulled the covers off her lap, and kicked her feet out. "You know I'd do anything to help you. You don't even need to ask."

"You know, you need to stop that," I told her, getting up.

"Stop what?"

"This 'I owe you so much' stuff," I told her. "It's kinda squicking me out after seeing Devana follow Ethel Elkins around and then try and kill someone. Just because the norn said so."

"Well, I wouldn't *kill* for you," Fortuna told me. "So, let's say I'd do *almost* anything to help you. But not anything. And it's not because I owe you. It's because you're my friend."

"Fair enough."

"One question, though—shouldn't we be trying to save Roland Makepeace? I mean, I know this is all important and all, but it seems like his life is hanging by a thread, here."

"I know, but Mercy knows that, too," I pointed out as we left her yurt together. "She's a powerful witch. Why is she over *here* and not over *there* trying to save him? Nothing was really happening over here. Gunther got taken over at the Makepeace Circus. Roland is sick at the Makepeace Circus."

"And yet she came here, looking for you," Fortuna mused. "You're right. That doesn't seem to make sense."

"No, it doesn't," I agreed. "And if I've learned one thing since coming here? When something nags at you? Figure it out before making a move."

CHAPTER 13

"WHAT'S THE PLAN?" GUNTHER ASKED WHEN I returned with Fortuna.

"I don't want to do anything with your dad until we fully understand what the heck everyone's agenda is," I told him.

"Do you think freezing Ethel Elkins and Devana was the *best* way to get to the truth here?" Kyle came over to Gunther and me. "Devana was the one that actually tried to kill him, and she *admitted* it. Seemed to me she was ready to talk. You didn't even give Ms. Elkins a chance to chime in."

"He has a point," Fiona agreed.

"In a normal situation out in the real world, you'd be right," I told Kyle. "But this *isn't* a normal situation. We know what the two of them were trying to accomplish—Roland's death. We don't know *why* they were trying to accomplish it."

"Then we should *ask* them," Kyle insisted.

"Mina World took Gunther over. She *claimed* she was just taking advantage of an opportunity that presented itself," I explained to Kyle. "What if she *wasn't*, though? What if Mina and Mercy knew what was happening and that's why they both showed up here?"

"How would they know?" Fiona asked, confused.

"They would know if they were in cahoots with Ethel Elkins," I told her.

My assertion dropped like a bomb in the center of the group.

"You can't be serious," Fiona gasped.

"Ethel Elkins working with the Witches' Council? I admit she's been a bit cagey and difficult at times, but that's a serious accusation." Gunther shifted uncomfortably. I stared at him in shock.

"Devana tried to *kill* your father," I told him.

"And she hasn't been unsuccessful yet," Fortuna said quietly.

"Hey, guys—" Aidan said.

"No, but we still don't know why she did what

she did." Gunther gazed back at his mother. "I agree with Kyle, I'm not sure freezing her was the best play here."

"Hey, Gunther, I can—" Aidan said as he turned toward my boyfriend.

"You don't shut up a witness and stop them from talking," Kyle interrupted. We continued huddling in a circle. "I mean, it's ridiculous. Crimes are crimes, paranormal or human. I don't see why we should handle this any differently than we would handle a regular case out in the—"

"FOLKS!" Aidan shouted.

"Jeez, dude, take a chill pill," Kyle said. We all turned to stare at Aidan.

"Mercy *was* here to turn on the Witches' Council." Aidan sighed now he had finally captured our attention. "Then she realized that Devana was responsible. Which meant that Mina was *not* responsible."

"Which meant that Mina never broke her oath to Mercy," I said. Aidan nodded.

"Once she outed Devana, she took action. As we spoke about it all, I read her and was able to see why Mercy remained after determining Mina didn't harm Roland at all," Aidan said. "Well, there may be more reasons, but I could see what she had done."

"Okay, so spit it out," I said. We waited.

Aidan closed his eyes and took a deep breath. Upon opening them, he stared into my eyes. They were filled with sadness and concern.

"She took Samson, Charlotte," Aidan said. "Samson's gone."

"Where is my cat!" I demanded from the Witches' Council witch.

Mercy crouched with her legs bent, hands up in a defensive posture. "Your cat is safe," Mercy said calmly. "I intend the guardian no harm, but I have no intention of getting shoved back to Impy by your stupid ringmaster powers before I have my say. Listen to me, and I will return him to you."

"Okay, no shove back to Imperatorial City. How do you feel about a baseball bat to the head, then?" I charged toward her angrily. Kyle, Gunther, and Aidan pushed hard against me to keep from lunging at the woman. I was astounded at the strength they mustered to keep me from moving. I was a tank, and I tried to calm myself down, so I didn't hurt them.

Samson? Samson!

Silence. Emptiness.

"Oh, my friend, what have you turned into," Gerda whispered sadly, her hands twisting in front of her. The specter was helpless to do anything but watch.

"This is a division, Gerda, and it will tear this world apart!" Mercy told her. "You know nothing about the Witches' Council or the agenda we operate under. You and your ilk have learned nothing in two hundred years!"

"We *know* that you've killed people," I spat at her.

"*I* have killed no one," Mercy answered defiantly.

"Your supposed best friend is standing right there, and she's a *freaking ghost!*" I hollered, pointing at Gerda over Gunther's shoulder. "Her husband is lying on his deathbed as we stand here! You kidnapped my cat! You think because a lightning strike from your hand didn't take a life, that somehow makes you *innocent* in all this?"

"I am *not* innocent, it is true, if we all bear responsibility for our *side*," Mercy's face twisted angrily. She stepped closer to me and shook her finger in my face. I jerked against the men holding me back and felt all three wince in pain. "But if we are blamed for the sins of the company we keep, then neither are *you*. You, then, are *responsible* for the peril Roland Makepeace finds himself in. *You*, Ringmaster. Not I, and *not* the Witches' Council."

I raised my hand in frustration, gathering power to push her back to that viper's nest of a city she came from. The energy rose and fell and rose and fell within me. I fought my desire to banish her from my sight and the realization that once I did so, Samson could be gone forever. I shrieked loudly in frustration amid the barrage competing desires fighting it out within my brain pulsed through my hand.

"I didn't ask for this war!" I told her angrily. "*You* did. You and Mina and Mabel showed up here, in my circus, and demanded I hand my circus over to you!"

"This is a war that *didn't* need to be fought," Mercy told me. I continued to stare at her angrily. "Our Master and Mistress are having an argument through us. We must stop mimicking their anger and their resolve to win at all costs. If we continue to fight a war against one another, one will win, and one *must* lose, Ringmaster. But if that happens, mark my words, we will all lose something that we can never get back!"

"What the *heck* are you prattling on about?"

Fiona stood off to the side and eyed Mercy with suspicion and fear, but Mercy's words had intrigued the kelpie.

"My master, Eiggam, controls the stability of the world. He is the spirit of all things fixed, all things steady, all things unchanging," Mercy told Fiona, her eyes flicking to the one member of our party that seemed to be listening to her. "He is untiring, unchanging, and unalterable. It is that stability we fight for."

"I guess opposites *do* attract because Maggie sure isn't *any* of those things," Fiona told her.

"She is not," Mercy said. "She is flighty, changeable, constantly mutable and unpredictable. The goddess is temperamental, haphazardly bouncing from place to place and idea to idea. Without stability, she is capricious and erratic."

"Without adaptability, Eiggam is rigid," I argued.

"Yes! Yes, written in stone!" Mercy shouted in triumph, nodding. "They *need* each other. Don't you understand? They *need* each other. Without one another, without compromise—"

"There's no evolution," Aidan said.

"You understand now," Mercy nodded. "With Eiggam, nothing ever changes."

"With Maggie, nothing can be counted on to stay the same," I said quietly.

"If either one of us truly wins, Ringmaster, it will be a catastrophe," Mercy pronounced. She lowered her hands and stood up. "A catastrophe for the world, both paranormal and human. The world will lack—"

"Balance," I finished, thinking of Devana. "There's no balance."

I nodded to the men holding me back forcefully, and each one backed away. I tried not to chuckle as each congratulated themselves for their *manly* strength. They held back the most powerful witch in the world, and because they did, each was duly impressed with himself.

I decided not to let them know I could have snapped every one of them like twigs.

"Why come to me?" I asked her. "I mean, you've clearly chosen a side here. Why not talk to Mina? Convince her of your theory? Get her to *stop* killing people?"

"I have tried," Mercy said with a sigh. "I have done so for near twenty years now. Eiggam promises a world unchanging. That means power once achieved is power *retained*. Permanently. Mina is tantalized by the idea of a world that she will control forever."

I glanced at Fortuna and raised an eyebrow. Fortuna nodded.

Mercy was telling the truth. At least a truth she believed, in any case.

"Mercy?"

"Yes?"

"My cat, please?" The witch eyed me warily.

"How do I know you will not simply banish me?"

"I will not shove you back to Impy. But I'm not going to continue a conversation like this while the guardian of the Magical Midway is being held hostage by you. If you mean what you say and you really want our help, trust has to start somewhere. My cat. Now, please."

After a few moments of consideration, Mercy nodded and waved her hand.

Samson appeared in the center of the room, his fur raised all over his body in such dramatic fashion that the poor thing looked like he'd stuck his paw in a light socket. His black eyes were wide, and he was panting.

Are you okay?

THAT TOOK YOU LONG ENOUGH! Samson shouted in my mind and raced to hide under the bed. The pillows shuddered as the cat shook.

She didn't hurt you, did she?

I AM NOT TALKING TO YOU!

"He'll be fine," I told Gunther.

Gunther eyed the bed and nodded, unconvinced.

~

"I do not agree with your side," Mercy said while everyone in the room slowly made their way to the seats at the center. "But I do not agree with mine. There is wisdom in both, but if I *must* fight, I will have to honor my oaths. As a witch, I cannot do other than that."

"Even if it means that my husband is *killed*?" Gerda asked. The ghost remained standing at the edge of the group, Anna at her side.

"Death is not always the end in our world, Gerda," Mercy told her, looking up.

"That's no excuse not to care," Gerda responded.

"Just because I care does not mean I will not do what must be done," Mercy told her friend sternly. Gerda's old friend tilted her head, and a small smile turned up the corner of her mouth. "I was concerned about the oath broken and saw the opportunity to try and avoid calamity. After what I witnessed here, I am not entirely sure that your husband's time has not come."

"You laugh at my husband's death?" Gerda gasped. "You are not the friend I knew!"

"How *are* you able to sit here and talk to us about this?" I asked Mercy. "I mean, as soon as you go back to Impy, won't Mina know where you've been? What you've told us?" I leaned forward and raised my eyebrow. "Or are you not going back?"

"I must return, but Mina will be unaware of all that transpired here. We are within the grounds of a circus, and thus we are in Maggie's domain. Mina, Eiggam...they cannot see within here. They are blind to the circuses. To you."

"Wow, that's one *heck* of a marital spat." Fiona leaned back in her chair. "Wait a minute... Charlotte was right, then? Maggie couldn't even see that you were here in this room, could she?"

"She could not, nor would she be able to see Mina or Mabel if they were here. That is why they need us to fight," Mercy explained.

"I don't understand," I said.

"Maggie and Eiggam are so angry at one another that they have blocked one another. They cannot see each other, speak to each other." Mercy waved her hands over the coffee table. Two people, a male and a female, shimmered like little dolls standing at either edge. "They have each chosen their champions, and they have taken their sides," she said as people popped up around them. Three witches that looked like Mina, Mercy, and Mabel appeared in front of the Eiggam figure.

In front of Maggie, there was Devana, and me.

"Wait a minute, why do *you* get three and we only get two?"

"You *should* have three," Mercy said looking at Gunther. "If Roland passes away, I suspect your company will be complete at that time."

"Now, wait a minute—" Gunther protested.

"There are no more minutes to wait, young Gunther," Mercy told him, cutting him off. Turning back to me, Mercy continued. "You may have only two champions, but if it comes to a final battle, Maggie will lose if you remain with two."

One, really. I had the other one frozen in jail, and she tried to kill Roland.

So, there was that.

"What about all these other people that Ethel Elkins keeps claiming are destined for this, that, and the other? There are more than three people that have claimed to be part of the prophecy," I pointed out to her. "Or Ethel Elkins herself. What's she, then?

"We have others as well," Mercy agreed. "They are *not* champions. They are important, but not essential. Each champion has a role in the balance of the battle, in the information that each side is to have, but the others are not essential. They do not turn the tide."

"For unicorn's sake, woman, *what* battle?" Fiona asked with exasperation. Ningul reached out a hand to Fiona's arm.

"The battle that is inevitable unless we find a way to avoid it," Mercy told her.

"Okay, so what happens if one of us wins?" I asked her.

"Then the world will either stagnate in darkness unable to evolve, or it will evolve randomly with no purpose," Mercy responded.

"And why should I believe you?"

"Because she's telling the truth," Fortuna spoke up for the first time since we all sat down. "She's being completely candid with you. She's holding some things back, but on the whole, what she's telling you is what she truly believes."

"It's a trick," Gerda told me. "She's *completely* different. This is not the Mercy Lawdottir I once knew."

"People change, Gerda," Aidan said.

"Gunther!" Wayland Black raced into my yurt. His skin was pale, and his one huge eye was wide open. "You have to come, quick! Your father's taken a turn for the worse."

Gunther jumped up and raced after Wayland. Stopping himself nearly at the door, he turned back. "Charlotte, I don't have the ability to heal my father. What do I do?"

Time seemed to slow down. Everyone stared at me, waiting for a decision. He wasn't asking me as his girlfriend. He was asking me as a ringmaster.

The more information I got, the more confused I became. How could Devana be chosen by Maggie as a champion for "our side" only to go behind our backs and try to kill Roland Makepeace? Why was I sensing more truth from Mercy of the Witches' Council than I had got from Ethel Elkins? How did Aidan not know that Devana had tried t0—

"You knew!" I accused Aidan as I remembered his temper tantrum on the way to the Makepeace Circus. "You knew that Devana was the one that poisoned Roland Makepeace! How could you not tell me?"

"I...I wanted to...I just," Aidan's eyes darted

around the room as if looking for an escape from my accusation. His shoulders slumped when Kyle stepped away from him. "I couldn't. I wanted to, but I knew that I couldn't. Some knowledge has to be earned, Charlotte. There are some things I can't say."

"That's *bloody well convenient*, then, isn't it!" I exploded at him. Standing up, I pushed the coffee table out of the way with a kick and stomped up to push him. Hard. "With all that we've been through, *you* let me run around like a chicken with my head cut off? Going in circles trying to figure this out? *And you knew the whole time!*"

"Charlotte, I—"

"Shut up! Just shut up! Not another word from you!" I told him.

I made my decision.

I turned and looked at Gunther. "Go with Wayland, get Ambom, and the three of you bring your father right to the edge of the Makepeace Circus grounds. I mean *right to the edge*! The same place where we joined the circuses before. And I'm not kidding - I want his toe scraping the boundary!"

Gunther nodded, and he and Wayland fled.

"What are you going to do?" Fiona asked hesitantly.

"Join the circuses," I told her as I stomped toward the front door. "Then I'm going to yank him across as fast as I can and save him."

"But what if—" Fiona started.

"The next person that tells me to let Gunther's father die will be in the same cell with Devana and Ethel!"

I stormed out before anyone else could say a word.

CHAPTER 14

N<small>O ONE FOLLOWED ME</small>. M<small>Y HEART THUMPED IN MY</small> chest as I ran to the edge of the boundary and stared across the small space left between the two circuses. I didn't have to move a dying man across a fairgrounds, and so I arrived in advance of Gunther.

I didn't know if what I was about to do was what I was supposed to do, but I knew it was the right thing to do. I wasn't a murderer, and I wasn't going to let someone die without trying to save him.

"Ringmaster," Patches Timbo greeted me quietly as he walked around the edge of the boundary. "Are you all right? You look a little worse for the wear."

"Hi, Patches," I said distractedly, my eyes scanning into the Makepeace Circus. "It's just been a long night. What are you doing up this late?"

"Late?" he asked, surprised. "This is my morning walk. I like taking one around the Magical Midway every morning just after the sun rises."

"Right, morning," I muttered, glaring at the rising sun. "Like I said, it's been a long night. I haven't been to bed yet. As soon as I am done here, I'll probably crash."

"And what are we doing here?" Patches asked, straining his powerful neck. The big man followed my gaze into the Makepeace Circus, but in the early morning light, all was quiet. The Makepeace Circus apparently did not rise at the crack of dawn.

"Roland Makepeace is sick," I told Patches. "I'm waiting for Gunther and their security guys to bring him to the edge of the circus so I can join them together and pull him across. Hopefully, once he's here, I'll be able to heal him."

"Why join the circuses?" Patches asked.

"It just seems the fastest way to get him across."

"My trunk is *certainly* long enough to reach

across that small a divide." Patches considered the small space between the two circus boundaries. "If they could hold his leg up, I could grab him and yank him across faster than you humanoids could carry him even with the two fairgrounds joined together."

"Are you sure?"

"Young lady," Patches scoffed, offended. "My trunk can lift over seven hundred pounds. It has almost forty thousand muscles. There is very little that my trunk cannot do. Also, I am a bull elephant.," Patches stood taller and straighter. "My trunk *dwarfs* the trunks of lesser males," he told me proudly.

"I, um…I'm sure you have a very nice trunk," I told him with not a small level of discomfort for no apparent reason as we discussed Patches' profligate trunk size. "If you'd be willing to help, that would be great. That would leave me to focus just on Roland and healing him."

"Absolutely," Patches nodded. I looked away for a moment as Gunther, Ambom, and Roland came into view. When I looked back, Patches had shifted into a gigantic elephant with long tusks and an impressively long trunk. He moved from side to side, waving his big gray ears, while we waited for the group to make its way over.

Patches' gentle eyes seemed impossibly small for such a massive creature.

"What's with the elephant?" Gunther called when he was about 100 feet away.

"We're not going to join the circuses," I shouted back. "Patches is going to yank your dad across with his trunk. Maybe that will buy us a few more seconds before whatever it is that's threatening him kicks in!"

Gunther nodded.

My boyfriend was levitating his father with great care, walking as if he were balancing a tray of overfilled wine glasses and hustling them steadily to impatient customers. Roland was lying flat, horizontal to the ground but level with Gunther's shoulder. Ambom walked on the other side of his ringmaster watching him with concern.

I could see from here why he was concerned. Blue bubbles frothed from Roland's mouth, and his body shook as if he had jumping beans under his skin.

"Is he still breathing?" I called. Patches gave a soft rumbling sound.

Gunther nodded without taking his eyes from his father.

"Can you pull him across from there? Like,

where he is floating?" I asked the elephant. Patches gave a cooing-rumble that sounded like a yes.

I hoped.

Gunther and Ambom took just a minute or two to bring Roland's floating, convulsing, frothing body right up to the edge of their fairgrounds.

"Everybody ready?" I asked. Ambom and Gunther nodded. Patches trumpeted and then extended his trunk to wrap around Roland's ankle. I extended my hand and got a bolt of levitation ready to catch him as he came through to the Magical Midway. "Okay, here we go. One… two…three!"

Patches yanked, I caught, and Roland suddenly gasped violently for breath.

"Dad!"

Magic blue beams exploded from my right hand while my left held the ample body aloft. As quickly as I could, I drenched him in the blue light and wanted to scream with excitement when his chest extended and he gulped a huge breath of air into his lungs. "That's right, Roland, breathe! Breathe!"

He gulped again, and again as Patches and I slowly lowered him to the ground. Color flooded back into his face, and the frothy blue stuff that had been bubbling to his mouth crystallized and dried, clinging to his chin like the remnants of cotton candy.

His eyes snapped open.

"It took you long enough!" he coughed when he came to rest on the ground. Sitting up, he glared at me. "How could you leave me like that! What were you doing, having a meeting about whether to let me die?"

"I...well, see, it's not what you think—"

"Dad, are you all right?" Gunther asked, kneeling down next to his father. "Do you need more healing?"

"I need a wet rag, that's what I need!" Roland complained and wiped his chin hard. "What is this wretched stuff? It tastes awful!"

"That's the taste of death!" Cama squeaked. I looked up and saw the death bat hovering over us all. "It's pretty sticky, but I think it tastes like molasses myself."

"You stay away from his hair!" I told her. She chuckled and flew in a loop.

"You have a death bat? What kind of crazy circus are you running here, girl?"

Patches Timbo looked up and jumped when he spotted Cama. After trumpeting an outrageously loud alarm that just about exploded my eardrums in my head, the huge elephant ran off toward the elephant pens. I made a mental note to go thank him for his help later.

Without Cama.

"You're welcome, Mr. Makepeace," I told Roland Makepeace cheerily. Gunther helped his father up.

"Like I said, it certainly *took* you long enough," he grumbled and dusted the dirt off of his jodhpurs. Gunther tried to help dust off his father, but the grumpy man pushed his son's hands away. "I'm fine! I don't need any help. This is humiliating enough as it is."

Gunther stepped back.

"Didn't you feel me grab on to you when you first came to check me out?" Roland barked at me. "Why didn't you just give a good yank so I could have at least come out and told you what was happening?"

"I could do that?" I asked.

Roland glared.

"Sorry, didn't realize," I apologized.

"What did they poison?" he barked.

"Your mouthwash," Gunther told him. "It was a death plant."

"A death plant, no wonder my mouth tastes like a desiccated mummy straight from the Sahara desert." Roland finished straightening his clothing. "A wet rag, Charlotte? Surely you can manifest that much."

So much for Roland's better disposition since I turned Gunther into a full witch and solved his circus's continued existence threat. I held out my hand and manifested a washcloth damp with water and scented with lavender. Roland snatched it from my hand and scrubbed the sticky residue of his poisoning off his face. Pulling it back, he sniffed and made a face. "What am I, a maiden?" he mocked.

I snapped my fingers and drenched the rag in eucalyptus. As Roland pulled the cloth back to his face, he gasped as the menthol stung his nostrils. He glared at me.

I glared back.

Then he chuckled. "You have some spirit to you, girl. I'll give you that."

"Dad, we really need to—"

"Just one more second, Gunther, I'm almost done," Roland told him, and he buried his face again in the minty-fresh washcloth.

"You did it!" Fiona called as she walked up upon the group with many others in tow. "I'm glad. Ningul and I were talking and we quite like ol' Roland. Would be a shame not to have him around anymore. He makes our ringmaster seem—"

"I make your ringmaster seem like an idiot," Roland said into his washrag. "I've been doing this longer than anyone else, and I'm great at it. I would have saved Charlotte in all of twenty minutes, and I wouldn't have needed an elephant—"

Somewhere in the middle of Roland's speech about how much better a ringmaster he was than me, he had removed his face from the washcloth. He raised his eyes and blinked once, then twice, trying to focus his eyes on the crowd so he could look at Fiona.

As the stinging eucalyptus faded, Roland's eyes found Gerda.

He grew silent and stared.

The rest of us smiled, watching the husband and wife as they gazed at one another for the first time in twenty years. Maybe more. Maybe less. But a long time. Gerda's face shone and sparkled with excitement. Roland's face was frozen in shock.

"Dad, this is what I was trying to tell you," Gunther said.

Roland stared at the woman he loved. He couldn't move.

"She's been here for years, Dad. They cast a spell so she couldn't get back to the Makepeace Circus, or Impy. So she stayed here, waiting..."

Roland didn't move.

Roland didn't breathe.

He just stared.

"Roland, my love," Gerda whispered. "I have waited so long to see you. I have missed you. I have missed you so much."

Roland didn't move.

Roland didn't breathe.

His hands shook.

"Is that Gunther's daddy, Momma?" Anna asked as she hid behind her mother. Gerda nodded yes but didn't answer the little girl. "Is he going to be my daddy, too, now, like Gunther is my brother?" Gerda hushed the little girl without looking down, continuing to lock eyes with her long-lost husband while patting Anna's head.

Roland didn't move.

Roland didn't breathe.

His hand dropped the washcloth to the ground.

"Dad, are you okay?" Gunther asked, his face tightening as he looked at his father.

"He's just had a wee bit of a shock, is all," Fiona told Gunther.

"Roland, say something," Gerda whispered.

Roland didn't move.

Roland didn't breathe.

His hand clutched his chest, and he collapsed to the ground.

"You have *got* to be kidding me," I said to no one in particular. I stared at the pale, motionless Roland laying dead at my feet.

CHAPTER 15

WE ALL JUMPED TO ACTION. GERDA SCREAMED, Fiona shouted, Gunther dove down to try and shake his father awake. Gerda's scream brought my Uncle Phil, and he pounded on Roland's chest. I let loose with a double blast of blue light from both my hands so powerful it felt like I was pulling energy from the earth itself.

Roland continued to lay there.

We worked, shaking him and hollering and pounding on his chest, I bathed him in blue…but it was pointless.

Roland was gone.

"Where *is* he, though?" I asked Gunther a half an hour later when we had given up. I looked around expecting that the ghost would pop out next to us, but he didn't. Reaching out toward him, I could tell he was no longer there. I didn't even know how, I just did. His body was a shell. "Did he really just move on without staying to say anything to Gerda? What kind of a jerk is your father, anyway?"

"Charlotte!" Uncle Phil whispered harshly.

Okay, maybe it was unfair, but we paranormals had a lot more choices than most people, and I couldn't believe Roland just disappeared like that.

How did he even disappear like that? How could he have died? We were indestructible! Ingesting poison only, right? At least, that's what I'd been told.

Gunther shook his head no, tears shimmering in his eyes.

I didn't know if he was answering my thought, or…suddenly I felt like a jerk. Gunther was gutted. I could feel it. As I moved toward him, my uncle grabbed my arm.

"Charlotte," Uncle Phil said as he pulled me away from Gunther and Roland. Far enough away, at least, that Gunther couldn't hear what Phil was saying.

"I'm sorry, I just don't understand where he is," I told Uncle Phil. "I should have realized that

Gunther would be grieving. Sometimes I don't think before I talk."

"I can see that," Uncle Phil said quietly as I continued staring. "I need you to focus on what I'm saying to you now. Charlotte. Charlotte! Look at me."

I snapped around at the urgency and demand in my uncle's voice. His face was grim.

"Roland's spirit is back at the Makepeace Circus. He's back there because he's waiting for the new ringmaster. So the power can be passed. Do you understand what I'm saying, Charlotte?"

I stared at Uncle Phil and shrugged. "So, Gunther's got to go and become ringmaster, big deal," I told him. "I did it. I mean, it's not *exactly* pleasant, mind you, but it's not a horrible experience as far as experiences go—"

"Charlotte, please," Uncle Phil said sadly, a heaviness weighing on him. He didn't want to say what he was about to have to tell me. My uncle was heartbroken over it, in fact. No, he thought I would be heartbroken over it. He was worried as he spoke again. "And then he will have to go back to—"

"The Makepeace Circus," I gasped as the reality of what was happening began to dawn on me. It felt like a punch in the gut. "He can't stay here anymore."

"No, my niece, he can't," Uncle Phil said sadly, his hand reaching to comfort me. As Gunther knelt beside his father's body, we could both see grief and anger and resentment and sorrow all fighting for preeminence on his face. "Your relationship is about to change, dramatically. Gunther is probably having a hard time with that at the moment, Charlotte. He loves you very much."

"I...oh, Uncle Phil..." My eyes filled with tears. "Why couldn't I have saved him?"

"My guess? It *really* was his time," Uncle Phil said quietly. "The other possibility is that he loves Gerda so much that Roland decided he wanted to be with her more than anything, and he was powerful enough to bring that about. Despite that old coot's arrogance, he knows Gunther can take care of the circus."

Delilah raced from the direction of my yurt, Samson following her slowly. The little cat jumped up on Roland's chest, turned toward Gunther, and meowed consolingly. Gunther petted the small cat, closed his eyes and bowed his head.

She's going to urge him back now, Samson said.

You should, as well. I know that this will hurt, Charlotte, but he must go. The quicker, the better. We are vulnerable. He must go and take up the ring.

Shut up, Samson.

Charlotte—

I walked away from Uncle Phil and pushed Samson out of my mind. Suddenly, I felt heavy. Weighted. Like the world was sitting on my shoulders and I would have to carry it alone from now on.

"*Never* that, love," Gunther whispered as he raised his pained face. "Things may change, but you'll never be alone."

"I don't want them to change," I said.

"Then perhaps you should defect to Eiggam's side." Gunther smiled at me tightly. Within seconds, his face fell again. "I don't know what I'm going to do without you, Charlotte."

"Hey, come on." I wiped the tears from my face and took a deep breath. Walking over, I knelt beside him and placed a hand on his back. "We still have the lawgiver bond. You can talk to me any time, you know. I'll visit. You'll visit. We'll work it out."

"It's not the same," he answered.

He was right.

"No, I guess it's not."

We sat quietly next to one another. Gunther's sadness and despair were so deep, I felt like I was drowning in it. After several minutes, he reached for my hand, and I turned to stare into his eyes. Eyes that knew me so well. Eyes I needed.

"Thank you," Gunther said sincerely, a catch in his voice. "All my life, I have been alone. Even when I wasn't alone, I *felt* alone. Ever since my mother left me," he said, nodding toward Gerda. She watched us silently, holding Anna tightly. "You have made me realize what a gift it is, what a beautiful thing it is, to not be alone. No matter what happens from here, I will always be grateful to you for that."

I tried to ask him why what he was saying sounded so final, so much like an ending, but he leaned forward and kissed me. Questions I had were lost in his gentle, chaste kiss. As Gunther pulled away, he grabbed Delilah and slipped her into his pocket. Pushing himself to his feet, my boyfriend kissed me once more on the forehead on the way up and then stood. He gazed slowly at each one of us.

"You have been good to me, and I thank you," Gunther said as he met the eyes of each one of my family. "You were the first people to make me feel like I truly belonged somewhere." Everyone murmured in response and nodded to Gunther, shocked at the turn of events and unsure of what to say.

"It won't be the same around here without you, Gunther," Aidan said.

"Take care of her. She may *seem* indestructible, but she is not." He turned and stared intently at Fiona and Ningul. "If there is ever anything that she needs that requires another ringmaster, I expect you to send word *immediately*. Swear to me that you will."

"Aye, Ringmaster, we will do so," Fiona whispered, tears rolling down her red cheeks. Gunther winced as she called him ringmaster, but he nodded to accept her oath and her naming of him.

"I take your oath as a kelpie, and I hold you to it," Gunther said. His voice was stalwart, he was sure of himself, and his statement radiated with power.

"Gunther, please—" I felt a sob catch in my throat.

"I *love* you, Charlotte Astley," Gunther said and he smiled again. "Always remember that. I will love you forever."

"Wait, please—"

Let him go, Samson said as Gunther turned,

and every muscle in my body screamed to stop him. There must be something we can do. Put Roland back into his body. Have Jeannie wish him another body. Something!

But I don't want to!

I know you don't, Charlotte, Samson thought sadly. He leaped to my shoulder and wrapped his tail around my neck. *These are trying times, and many things will be sacrificed before it is all over.*

I hate this! It's too soon!

I am sorry, Samson thought unpretentiously. We watched the love of my life cross the barrier and leave the Magical Midway.

Gunther turned in the tiny space between the two circuses and looked back at me. I held my hand high, palm out, and sent all the love I felt for that quiet, gentle man toward him in a wave. His hand raised in return, and he smiled. "Always, Charlotte," he called.

Then he turned. His shoulders back, he pulled his head high and stepped onto the Makepeace Circus.

With a flash of enormous power, Gunther and the Makepeace Circus disappeared. I collapsed, weeping, into my uncle's open arms.

CHAPTER 16

I SAT IN THE SECURITY OFFICE AND STARED AT THE frozen women the lares had locked in our newly created jail. I'd been there for hours. Maybe days. Just staring at them.

Devana and Ethel Elkins.

Traitors.

At first, the lares guards had checked on me. Gallus, Lucius, Marcius, and Julius entered stiffly and asked "Anything?" periodically. It seemed like they came in every two or three hours, and each had visited me at least twice. I always nodded my head no, without taking my eyes from the two women, and eventually, they would leave. Bob encouraged me to go, to eat, to sleep, and I would refuse him, too.

Samson sat beside me on the desk, alert but silent.

The women stared back, but I didn't bother trying to figure out what they were thinking or feeling. I didn't care.

I was angry.

So angry.

And I was alone.

"I've about right had it with this nonsense, Charlotte," Fiona said, bursting into the security room. The door banged against the wall as she threw it open, the sun blinding me as it flooded the room. Anya, Avalon, and Fortuna followed behind her.

I glared at her. "Get out."

"Get stuffed."

"*What* did you just say to me?"

"I think you heard me, unless yer ears are stuffed from not sleeping for three days now," Fiona snapped. She banged a bag down on the counter. With single-minded purpose, she laid out a bottle of water, an apple, a slice of pizza, and a napkin. "Eat."

"Fiona, I'm busy—"

"No, you're *angry*," Fiona shook her head. "And I get why. Truly I do, and oh, Charlotte, my heart breaks fer ya and what yer going through.

But you've moped, stewed, and seethed long enough over what fate's done to you and Gunther."

"We're not going to let you continue like this until your rear end grows and attaches to that chair," Anya agreed. "You need to sleep, you need to eat, and you need to deal with the two of them."

I pushed the apple away. "What do you think I've been here trying to figure out?"

Fiona crossed her arms, and her eyes narrowed.

Okay, she was right. That was a lie. I hadn't been trying to figure anything out at all. I had been stewing. And moping.

And, okay, there was a fair bit of seething, too.

Perhaps it was what you needed, Samson said. *Your friends are correct, however. It is probably time to move past this.*

"Shut up, Samson," I said out loud as I pushed the pizza away.

"See, even the cat agrees," Fiona glared.

"Shut up, Fiona."

"If you keep doing this, Charlotte, she's going to get on the cauldron, and she's going to call your new, equally powerful ringmaster boyfriend." Anya picked up the water and slammed it down in front of me. "She's going to tell him how you're acting, and he's going to feel as bad as you *look*."

"You wouldn't!"

"She probably wouldn't, not quite yet," a voice called from the door. "But I would."

My eyes searched for the owner of the voice, and I came face to face with Roland Makepeace. Gunther's father walked in and asked my girl gang if he could speak to me alone. I thought Fiona would argue with him for a moment, but she reluctantly headed toward the door. "We'll be right outside," Fiona warned me to ensure I knew our little talk was not yet over.

Roland walked in and sat down across from me. He looked different. The Roland I knew had been tense, sarcastic, always a little gruff and a little angry. This Roland? This Roland exuded peace. Satisfaction.

Well, of *course* he did. He had his partner back.

And in doing so, he took mine away.

"My son would never forgive me if I let you go on like this too much longer, Charlotte." Roland leaned forward and looked at me kindly. "I promised him after his elevation that I would make sure that you were all right. I intend to keep that promise."

"I'm fine," I lied, and sat up straight. "I've just been in here thinking."

"Yes, I used to do that kind of thinking with whiskey," he confided knowingly. Roland picked up the water bottle and held it out to me, his ghostly hand sparkling. "You, I see, do it with self-destructive withdrawal from everyone and everything. Including eating and sleeping."

I snatched the water bottle from his hand, took a gigantic gulp, and then slammed it back down on the counter. Holding my hands up, I raised my eyebrow.

"It's a start, dear girl," Roland smiled sadly.

"Gunther's got his power now?" I asked, trying to change the subject.

"He does, and thanks to hanging around you these past months, he already had a good handle on what needs to be done." Roland smiled. He leaned back on the stool and turned his head to look at Ms. Elkins and Devana. "Haven't unfrozen them yet?"

"They tried to kill you!"

"Well, yes," Roland agreed. "But they didn't. And Ms. Elkins was right as usual. It *was* my time. Though I do wish that she had simply had a discussion with me about it instead of sneaking her huntress into my bathroom to poison my mouthwash." Roland shuddered. "Those death plant things are awful."

"How could it *possibly* have been your time?"

"Because I would never have been useful to you or Gunther the way I was," Roland admitted. It was clear the now-gentle man was somewhat embarrassed. "Gerda and I needed each other to be whole and complete, Charlotte. And you and Gunther needed us to be whole and complete in order to help you with what you both need to do. This was the only way."

"You don't know that," I snapped. I pointed my finger accusingly at Ethel Elkins, my hand shaking. "*She* didn't know that. They kept secrets and snuck around behind everyone's backs. Maybe we could have worked out what we needed to without your having to die—"

"But then Gunther would not be the only other living ringmaster—"

"Would that be so bad?" I teared up as I slammed back down on the chair and buried my head in my hands. "What would it have mattered *who* was the ringmaster as long as there were two?"

The pain stabbed at me again and I struggled not to break down weeping. As I tried to hide from all that was happening around me, I felt a pressure against my head. Then a harder force. Raising my face, Roland had moved in close and was watching me with an almost fatherly concern, his spectral hand caressing my hair.

"I'm not a young man, Charlotte." Roland leaned closer and spoke in a soothing rasp. With a fatherly caress, he smoothed my rat's nest of hair. "We may not die, but we do age. We do grow. Life takes its toll upon us. I would not have been a worthy partner for you during this time. My son is," Roland said. Then he sat back, and his voice grew stronger. "I could not have taken care of the Makepeace Circus, and been with Gerda—she is still barred from it. I would have had to choose between my responsibility and my wife—"

"So now Gunther has to choose between the Makepeace Circus and me?" I accused him as my mouth twisted.

Roland stared at me. "Or *you* must choose between the Magical Midway and *him*."

I blinked. The thought had never even crossed my mind.

And that, in the end, was Roland's point. My face grew hot as the pain twisted within me anew, now wracked with guilt that I never even considered leaving the Magical Midway for Gunther. Not once.

"Do not look so stricken, my girl," Roland chuckled. "You will not choose, and neither will Gunther. The world needs you both. We are ringmasters, and with our power comes responsibility. We sacrifice for it. It was my time to wield power, and then it was my time to pass it. Things have happened as they needed to."

I shook my head no and stared daggers at Ethel Elkins.

"Talk to her," Roland said simply. "Perhaps you will gain a better perspective."

I agree, Samson chimed in.

I whispered a truth spell, binding the two women to speak only the truth. I didn't compel them to answer my questions—I still wasn't comfortable enough to do that. But anything that they told me once I freed them from being statues would be the truth, at least as they understood it.

Once I could confirm the truth spell was in place, I took a deep breath and steeled myself to refrain from blasting them with a magic laser.

With a wave of my hand, I unfroze the traitors.

"About time!" Ethel gasped.

Don't! Samson cracked as I raised my hand to refreeze the arrogant old woman.

"You don't listen," the old woman said as she paced back and forth in the large cell. Devana had not spoken once since I had unfrozen her. Upon awakening, the huntress witch turned her back to me and knelt in the right edge of the cell on her knees. With her head bowed, and her face turned from me against the wall, she looked like a chastised child sent to the corner.

"You don't talk," I responded coldly. "If you had come to me and said 'Charlotte, Gunther needs to be elevated to ringmaster. Roland also needs to die, but he'll be pretty happy about it since he'll be moving in here to the Magical Midway with everyone else to be with the wife he thought he'd lost. You and Gunther should maybe get together and make a plan to maintain your relationship for when this happens, because it will certainly disrupt things.' Would any of those words, that honesty, have been hard to say?"

"If *you* were a better witch, you would have been able to *sense all that*," Ethel snapped and banged her cane against the bars. Her face twisted in frustration.

"So now this is all *my* fault?" My voice rose as I stood up. "*Your* pet murderess over there in the corner was *hurting* Fortuna just so no one would find out about your betrayal! And what about Maggie? I've been ringmaster *how long?*"

"Not long enough, apparently," Ethel snapped.

"But *I* was, Ms. Elkins," Roland told her calmly. "And so was Phil. And neither one of us knew anything about Maggie or this prophecy. All the ringmasters remained divided for as long as we can remember, and yet we were all on the same side. We just didn't know it."

"You didn't need to know!" her expression hardened. "It wasn't about you! It was about the Thirteenth Witch!"

"No, it was about our children and our families," Roland disagreed. "You've been withholding information from us for years, Ethel. Charlotte has every right to be suspicious of you."

"What do you have to say for yourself?" I called to Devana in the corner. "She may be pulling strings. But *you* did it. Were you ever going to tell me?"

Devana's shoulders raised once as if she was taking a deep breath, and then her head bowed even more profoundly. With an elegant grace, the woman leaned forward and pushed herself up. "I would have told you when I had leave to tell you, Charlotte," Devana's voice echoed against the wall she faced. Slowly, she turned and met my eyes. "I told you once that I serve the balance."

"You told me once that you were more or less her *slave*," I snapped, pointing at the old woman. Devana shook her head no vigorously.

"I told you I was not free," she disagreed. "That is not the same thing."

"Explain it to me."

She squeezed her eyes shut. Her breathing was pained, labored. Not quite as labored as Roland's had been as he lay dying in his cabin, but enough that I seemed to feel the tension in her muscles. Ethel Elkins watched her with interest.

"It is *my* people's fault," she said, her voice thick with sorrow. "This division between Eiggam and Maggie. It is the huntress witches that precipitated their rift. It is we who caused the withdrawal of magic. All of this? It is our fault," she admitted.

For the next two hours, Devana explained how the fight between Eiggam and Maggie got started. How their anger and mistrust was stoked. How the two beings' anger toward one another was manipulated in the pursuit of power. How one huntress witch's intent to sow division within the paranormal world to gain power was ultimately successful, and how she, Devana, had volunteered to sacrifice her life if called for to heal what a member of her clan had broken.

"I am *willingly* bound to this pursuit," Devana explained. "While it is true that I am not free, it is a servitude I accepted willingly to restore the balance to the world. My people owe it for the stain of sin on our clan."

"How did serving the balance become *blindly* following whatever Ethel Elkins' told you to do?" I asked an exhausted Devana. Her story was compelling, fascinating—one of her own, thirsty for power, had manipulated all of this? It seemed crazy, and yet I had seen some strange things since becoming ringmaster, so it didn't seem all that farfetched. Despite all she had told me and Roland, her blind devotion to the old woman still didn't make sense.

The huntress witch looked at the old woman and raised an eyebrow. Ms. Elkins's face was blank as she stared back at Devana.

"Ethel Elkins is the norn that attempted to stop the huntress witch from taking power." Devana turned back to face me. "Since her defeat, she has been working to ensure that the Thirteenth Witch would succeed where she failed."

"You've been *alive* since this all started?" I asked Ms. Elkins incredulously. "You were there before the circuses? When there were still lawgivers, when humans still had an inkling that there was magic in the world? You were *part* of it?"

She nodded once.

"Then that means you know who—"

"Mina World," Devana answered for her mistress. "Mina World is the huntress witch that started this all."

I freed them.

I made them oath that they would no longer make any moves behind my back going forward, and we sealed that pact with magic. After everything the two women had told me, Devana explaining and Ms. Elkins confirming, I couldn't blame them for what they had done. They had a deeper understanding of the situation than I did, and they were trying to do what was right.

They were just doing it the wrong way. That had to change.

I always realized it was serious. I did not know that I was merely the latest player to step on the field in a game going on for hundreds of years.

As I walked out of the security area, I waved to Fiona and let her know I had information I needed to get to Gunther. Fiona, Anya, and Fortuna had waited outside of that building for me for almost three hours. As I walked toward the communications yurt, I wondered what I did to deserve such incredible friends.

You're very lovable, you know, Gunther's voice popped up in my mind. My heart leaped in my chest as I looked around for him.

Are you here?

No, love, I'm at the Makepeace Circus, Gunther said. *Aidan mentioned that all lawgivers could call to one another even across distances. I must have it very quiet and concentrate a bit harder, but it works.*

I have so much to tell you—

I can still hitch a ride in your head, Gunther said as he cut me off, and I swore I could hear him laughing. *I heard everything that Devana said. That was quite a story.*

I stopped walking.

What do you think we should do now? I asked him.

I think everyone needs to hear this story, Gunther

said. *I need about another week or so to settle things here. Then we can move the circuses next to one another and have a meeting. I think we should send word for Scout Trout to join us since we have a relationship with him.*

What about the other were leaders? I asked him.

We haven't met them, Gunther responded. Nelly and Pack, two were-elephants, walked by and looked at me strangely. I nodded and smiled at them. *Our circus folks, between both grounds, cover most paranormals. They know their clans, so I think they can hear the information and decide what to do with it.*

Kyle and Fortuna can sit for the humans, I agreed.

The sun rose higher in the blue sky, and I felt the warmth on my skin. As I grew more powerful as a ringmaster and gained a better understanding of my powers and limitations, I knew now I could go days, maybe even weeks, with no food and no sleep. The only thing I had to have was water. It was the lifeblood of the earth. I wasn't sure if I had to have it to stay hydrated, or I had to have it to maintain my tie to the planet I walked upon, but I knew it was important.

So go get some water, and then get sleep, Gunther

said. *You may not need it, but I can sense your weariness.*

He couldn't. All we could do through our tie was talk.

But Gunther knew. Gunther knew me.

I miss you, I told him.

And I you, he responded.

I'll see you in a week?

We'll talk before that, Charlotte, Gunther chided. *I'm always right here.*

I sighed.

It wasn't good enough.

*Go grab **A Call to Charms**, the next book in the Magical Midway series right now!*

KEEP UP WITH LEANNE LEEDS

Thanks so much for reading! I hope you liked it! Want to keep up with me?

Visit leanneleeds.com to:

Find all my books…

Sign up for my newsletter…

Like me on Facebook…

Follow me on Twitter…

Follow me on Instagram…

Thanks again for reading!

Leanne Leeds

FIND A TYPO? LET US KNOW!

Typos happen. It's sad, but true.

Though we go over the manuscript multiple times, have editors, have beta readers, and advance readers it's inevitable that determined typos and mistakes sometimes find their way into a published book.

Did you find one? If you did, think about reporting it on leanneleeds.com so we can get it corrected.

www.ingramcontent.com/pod-product-compliance
Lightning Source LLC
Chambersburg PA
CBHW031941240626
47153CB00003B/818